Go Down Hard

Ali Seay

GRINDHOUSE
PRESS

For Jason.
Thank you.
{kiss, kiss}

ONE

JACK

IT WAS THE DUST THAT first caught Jack's attention. The farm was big, sprawling, and deserted. Just him and the chickens, so to speak. Only there were no actual chickens.

The closest house was the Myers house a piece up the road. It had been deserted since the old man died in 2017. The dust must be a realtor or a long-lost family member. Not that Jack thought the old guy had any. If he did, it had taken them long enough to show up.

He walked to the front window, pulled his binoculars from the sideboard, and patted Casey on the head. The black lab whimpered once, licked his hand, and pounded his big tail against the floor while his master gazed outward.

It was a pickup. A big beat up white one with a bunch of stuff bungee corded in the back. It was on the same level of epically fucked up as his red Jeep out in the side yard. He smiled. He had company.

It had been ages.

I

GO DOWN HARD

The truck farted smoke as the engine cut. The sudden silence a reminder of how noisy that behemoth had been careening up the main road.

He felt a stab of surprise when she hopped out of the cab. He'd been expecting a large good old boy, a lanky farm hand, or even some ancient coot who'd come to check out the large property. Instead, she stood there, shielding her eyes from the bright sunlight.

Her hair was short and choppy. Maybe black. She was just a tiny thing in the lens of his binoculars so he was unsure. Faded jeans hugged the trim flair of her hips and she wore a white wife beater with a black bra.

Slut-wear, his mother would have called it.

Jack just thought it was fashion. Nothing more. Nothing less. And looking at the newcomer and the way she carried herself—comfort.

She kicked up dust with her boots as she walked toward the wide, weathered front porch. It had been a while since they'd had rain.

She walked up the steps like she owned the place, and she very well may. A quick thrum of electric attraction hit him and he kept his binoculars trained on her.

She shoved both hands in her back pockets as she walked the length of the wooden porch. She toed the old aluminum glider and watched it rock creakily back and forth. Leaning over, she shielded her eyes and peeked inside. Then she walked to the very edge, peered over the railing, and into the weed and vine-tangled yard.

She was stunning. He could picture her at his table with him eating dinner. A nice chicken parm, garlic bread, salad. Okay, maybe not garlic bread, maybe just a nice loaf of good Italian bread. Girls—women, he corrected himself—could be funny about garlic on a first date.

2

And wine. Definitely wine. It wouldn't be a Jack West dinner without vino. Spiked, of course.

"Right, Casey?" he muttered.

Casey's tail thumped agreeably.

He continued to watch her. She pulled a key out of her pocket and tugged open the storm door. It was only on by one hinge so she had to grab it. She was laughing. She had a lovely smile. A long, thin, gorgeous neck and a clavicle men should want to worship with kisses. She fit the key into the door and entered.

"Either a realtor or a renter or an owner. We shall see," he muttered.

He shut his eyes briefly, picturing it perfectly. Pouring her a glass of wine. Pouring his own. Not drinking it, though. Just letting it sit there. Watching her drink. Watching her falter. Watching the realization hit.

He felt the heaviness between his legs but ignored it. He had recon to do.

What was her name, he wondered? Alice? Jane? Or something complicated or trendy? Britany? Monet? Bella?

She came out a moment later, propped the screen door open with a door stop from the porch, and went to the truck. She climbed onto the tailgate, moving very much like a farmhand or an athlete—he'd have to remember that—and undid the bungee cords. She grabbed a big duffle, then another, and hauled them into the house. She made a return trip, snagged some boxes, carrying two of them, one stacked atop the other. Her biceps popped, her delts, too.

This was getting more exciting by the minute.

He'd have to go introduce himself very soon. It was the neighborly thing to do.

TWO

MEG

SHE DROPPED THE DUFFLES IN the bedroom, the boxes in the kitchen. Her phone gave a little jingly burble but she ignored it. Dating apps. Constantly going off, usually for no damn good reason.

So far, she had yet to find the guy for her. Or even a guy fit for any woman, really.

"And yet, I persist."

She flipped open one of the boxes and pulled out a clothesline, some clothespins, an iron she never used, and various other things.

A glance out at the yard told her she'd been right. Barren, empty, one broken lawn chair, an old clothes tree for hanging, and what looked to have been a sandbox at some point. She wasn't sure if that would stay or go. She had time to decide.

She had to bang the wooden frame of the window to get it to give. She wrestled it up and sweet, clean air came flooding in along with the sounds of birds. She had a love-hate thing with birds. She

4

liked the predatory nature of them, but the sound of them chirping made her insane.

That made her think of her BB gun in the truck and that made her smile. Not that Meg would shoot a bird. Birds were innocent. Unless they chirped too much. Too early.

She kicked some dust bunnies out of her way as she went back out to the truck. The front door was still propped open to let some clean air in the dirty house.

She shielded her eyes and stepped back to stare at her new home. She had some decorating and cleaning up to do before it was fit for any of her online suitors. But she'd get it there.

She grabbed two more boxes from the bed of the truck and then the BB gun. She froze for a moment, not hearing anything, but *feeling it.* Like someone was watching her. She set her load down and spun slowly in a circle, shielding her eyes.

The only thing she saw was a house up on the hill. Across the road. Way up there. Looming. There were a bunch of outbuildings and what looked like an old RV, maybe a camper too. A lot of it looked old and dilapidated. Maybe a farm?

If anyone lived there, they had a lot of property to look after.

She stared for a moment longer. Then there it was, the wink of sunlight on a shifting lens. Someone was watching her. The hair on the back of her neck tingled. She laughed under her breath and gave a jaunty wave.

Then she turned and grabbed her stuff to carry the rest inside.

Her phone jingled again. There was Chris. Tall, thick, dark hair, scruff along his sharp jawline, dark blue eyes. He was cute. "I like spirited women. Women who like to please their man. Women who are feisty." He was a pretty boy, clearly. He wanted a woman who was DTF, that was for sure. She stared at his face, tapped her lip. Then smiled and hit the button for INTERESTED and waited.

Maybe he'd be her first visitor.

THREE

JACK

HE'D REARED BACK A LITTLE when she waved. He wasn't used to that. It was weird, someone picking up on what he was doing. It was hard to remember other people were perceptive while living out here amongst the nothingness.

He winked at Casey. Casey whined and thumped his tail.

"She saw me," he said, feeling slightly unnerved. "She waved to me."

Casey licked his lips.

He figured he should go visit very soon. Just to get a handle on his new neighbor. It was clear she was moving in now she'd dragged a bunch of stuff out of her truck.

Best to fix up the house. Invite her to dinner, maybe. That made his stomach tumble a little. The thought of her being here. Her in her faded jeans, her wife beater and black bra, her no bull-shit haircut, and cheeky wave.

The tension between his legs was back again. Time to occupy

6

his mind lest the devil get his hand in his pants. His mother would have beat him senseless.

Jack put the binoculars on the windowsill and found a broom, a dust pan, and some disinfectant spray. He went into the basement and opened the door to the cage. He swept and sprayed and checked the linens.

He might be having a new guest soon. Had to make sure everything was nice.

Then he went up through the kitchen and put on his sneakers. Jack didn't wear shoes in the house. They were dirty.

Casey followed him out back as he did a walk through. He visited the nice barn first, his shoes crunching across the dry grass. The nice barn was tidy and clean. Hay in bales. Farm implements oiled and hanging on walls. No livestock for Jack. The only things that visited his barns were human.

He shut his eyes, breathed deeply, and let the memories of the last girl to visit this particular building run through his head. The smell of her long blond hair—when he first brought her home and then later, when she'd been there a while. In the beginning it smelled like peaches, in the end it smelled like hay and pennies.

She had the sweetest cries. Her name had been Polly and she was buried back by the large rocks at the bend of the shallow creek.

A plane flew overhead and his eyes snapped open. He walked to the wall and found a pick axe. He'd wrapped a few strands of her lovely hair around the handle. For the sake of memory.

He touched it and resisted the urge to smell it. He stared down at the dog. "Come on, let's go to the old barn."

The old barn had been the main barn when his grandfather had owned the property. Time and elements and farm life are usually enough to dilapidate even the finest farm. His grandfather had kept the old barn standing for his cars. He'd had a thing for cars of all kinds—old, new, foreign. He also had a thing against the

7

county they lived in, so if the excess of vehicles were under cover, no inspectors could come sniffing around.

Inside the barn were the ones Jack had kept when the property finally became his. A VW Beetle from the sixties—butter yellow with a nice case of rust leprosy. An old Chevy van with porthole windows in a shade of shocking cobalt blue. It had no seats in the back. Just two captain's chairs up front. There was a '66 Mustang Coupe—dirty white—that was more rust than car. And those were just his favorites.

He wondered which one his new neighbor would go for when he set her loose in here and maybe locked her in. Which one would she hide inside?

Jack smiled. It was decided. He *would* visit her. He would woo her. If it all went to plan, he'd wine and dine her, then he'd hunt her. And if he won the hunt, he'd kill her.

The dog turned and ran from the barn.

FOUR

MEG

I T DIDN'T TAKE LONG FOR her phone to ding.

"Hi, M, I'm Chris."

She nearly rolled her eyes. Yeah, no shit, Sherlock. Your profile says that.

She didn't say that, though.

She typed: Hi!!!

Exclamation points were important. Especially for a woman who "liked to please her man."

"I see you're interested ;) Maybe we should get a drink and see if we're a match? Would you like that?"

Meg glanced around the shambles of a house. Nothing was ready yet, but why not check it out? What could it hurt?

"Sure!! When did you want to meet?"

She hit send on the app and waited. A little swirling icon let her know Chris was, in fact, messaging her back.

"He's going to say tonight," she muttered.

"How about tonight?"

She smiled. Now she'd see just how big of a prick pretty boy Chris was.

"Oh, I can't tonight. I could tomorrow. How about that?"

She put the phone in her pocket and began to unpack. She put all the stuff from the utilities box in the cabinets under the kitchen sink. The place had come fully furnished, which she liked.

The kitchen table was old, heavy, solid wood, and long. The chairs were equally substantial and made of weathered but good wood. She scrubbed the floor on hands and knees, all the while working in silence.

No ding from her phone, just the sound of her breathing and working.

She found herself humming as she cleaned the table and the chairs with sanitizing wipes. No reason she couldn't be clean in her work space. She wiped down the sink and the countertops. She looked in the fridge, which was running, and found it clean and bare.

She wiped it down anyway. Best to *know* it was clean and not just assume.

She vacuumed out the dresser drawers, also made of nice sturdy wood. A darker wood. Chestnut maybe?

Once she knew they were clean, she put her clothes away. She stripped the bed of linens, vacuumed the mattress, and put her own sheets on.

All told, she worked for an hour and a half in silence, getting her home ready for future company.

She found herself hot and sweaty but pleased.

Her phone finally dinged.

"I guess that's okay. You're near Baltimore it says? How about Miss Vick's? Seven?"

She was not near Baltimore anymore. She was out in the sticks, just as she wanted. But he didn't need to know that.

"Sure. That's great. See you then."

She rolled her eyes and tossed her phone on the bed as she stripped off her dirty, sweaty clothes. When he hadn't gotten his way, he'd pouted and punished her, making her wait a long time for a response. Then he made it feel like he was doing her a favor by answering.

She grinned at herself in the bathroom mirror as she turned the water as close to scalding as she could without hurting herself.

Oh, she liked him. He was going to be fun.

FIVE

JACK

THE DOORBELL RANG, STARTLING HIM. He
wasn't expecting anyone. People rarely came here. Usually only when he found a new friend. It had been a
while. His last friend had occupied the cage.

Jack hurried to the door. He moved the ancient curtain covering the heavy, leaded glass of the front door. Callie smiled, gave
him a peppy wave.

He gave her a smile back. It took him a split second to craft
one, not that she'd have noticed. He let the curtain drop and unlocked the door.

What the hell was she doing here?

"Hey, Jack!" she said. "I was driving up to Sam Merkin's place
and I figured I'd stop by. We got that food you wanted for Casey.
No grains. So . . ." She shrugged and held it out.

He knew he should be neighborly. So, he smiled at her, took
the bag, and stepped back.

"Come on in," he said. Though her being in the house was the

12

last thing he wanted. He did a cursory glance around and found everything fine for her to come inside.

He moved toward the kitchen and felt her following. Casey, hearing a new voice, came trotting out. That was Callie's cue to get down on one knee and rub his big head vigorously, all the while accepting sloppy wet kisses.

"Such a good boy," she kept saying as Jack watched.

Casey had shown up as a stray. He thought having a dog would be a good idea for when he brought friends home. He thought it made him look complete. So, he kept Casey. Casey loved Jack as much as anyone could, Jack thought.

He was not easy to love.

"What do I owe you, Callie?" The prompt was to get her out.

He had cleaning and planning and thinking to do now the woman had moved in across the road. If he was going to make a move on her, it should be before anyone even realized she was there. Less suspicion.

Callie looked up and shrugged. It made her loose crop top slide down off her shoulder. He saw clearly she wasn't wearing a bra. The soft fabric of her top caressed her small tea cup-sized breasts. Her full nipples were clearly outlined.

He looked away. He didn't want to see that. He could hear his mother in his head, *She's probably unclean, Jack, don't mess with her* . . .

"Nothing. You can pay next time you come in. I was out here anyway and I figured I'd pop in so he could have his food as soon as possible. Because it's good for him, yes, it is," she said, the final sentence coming out as one long string of cooing baby talk.

"Well, thanks. That sure was kind."

She stood and gave him an awkward little bow. Callie was on the shy side. Her showing up like this was entirely unexpected and that threw him off. Jack didn't like to be surprised. He liked to be the one doing the surprising.

"How's the writing life going? Any new technical manuals lately?" She leaned against the door jamb.

Jack told different people different things. All of them boring. He'd learned the lesson from reading an article many years ago. A former CIA agent said that, when people asked, he told people he worked in a toll booth. Because no one ever asked any questions beyond that. It was too boring to care about.

Jack's go-to occupations—that could all be done simultaneously should people compare notes—were technical manual writer, proofreader, website developer, and reselling online. All of these things were believable, things he'd actually done at some point, and could do if anyone were to put him on the spot.

In reality, his mom had left him a sizeable estate, his grandfather had left him the farm, and he kept whatever happened to be on his guests at any given time.

It was a living.

"Fine. I had one for a blender."

"Oh, a big company?"

She was flirting with him. It hit him like a cotton wrapped fist. She was batting her lashes, shifting her stance, lowering her gaze in a coy way.

Jesus. This was uncomfortable.

"No. Some knock-off. No big deal. Listen, I have a lot of cleaning to get done."

"Company coming?" She looked a bit upset.

"No. Just OCD." He didn't smile when he said it. It wasn't entirely untrue. And maybe Callie would be turned off by such a thing.

No such luck.

She reached out and touched his arm gently. Jack had to focus on not flinching.

"I understand. I'll get going." She bent to give Casey one last pat, thus allowing Jack one last gaze down into the gaping maw of her loose top. Her small pink nipples were hard.

He looked away.

"I'll see you in town," she said.

He nodded and ushered her to the door. He didn't want to prolong the encounter but had to act like a normal person. "Sure, I can't pay you now for the chow?"

She turned and flashed her toothpaste ad smile at him. "I'm sure. I'll see you at the store."

He realized it was all designed to see him again. He'd have to make sure and call Bruce, the owner, and pay him via phone.

He'd have to let her cool off before he saw her again.

Plus, he had bigger things to worry about than her schoolgirl crush. Like the girl across the street.

SIX

MEG

SHE DROVE THROUGH HER OLD neighborhood to
get to Miss Vick's. She'd moved because things had gotten
too close for comfort there. Neighbors had ended up liking
her, knocking on the door, checking in, wanting to do dinner.
That sort of thing.

Meg wasn't a socializer by nature. She could count on one hand
how many people in her life she liked to be around. None of them
were family.

She brushed her hair out of her face. She'd put on some stunning makeup. Much more than her norm. Her eyes were done up
all smoky and vixen-like but her lips were a pale, blushing pink.
A mix of angel and demon for good old Chris. A bad girl who
knew how to be good. Much more interesting than a good girl
who knew how to be bad.

She walked in and did a quick scope of the place. Not too
crowded and not the kind of place where anyone was paying attention to anyone else. They were all focused on their drinks,

getting laid, or a festive combo of the two.

She found a table by the door that suited her. Meg had attempted to be here before him. Guys like him tended to like to make an entrance.

Fine by her. He could come after her if he wanted. Pun intended.

She smoothed down her black tank. A string of rough turquoise beads circled her throat. High up so they showed off her pulse point. Close fitted to the throat, almost choking, tended to appeal to the predatory men.

She had no doubt Chris was a predatory man. It rolled off him in oily waves, even through a phone app.

When the door flew open and warm summer air boiled into the cool bar, she knew it would be him. And it was.

Just like his app pics, which was all too often not the case. But he was way too proud of his body and his looks to be anything but exactly as handsome as his profile shot. Tall, at least six-four, thickly muscled. His rakish dark hair hung in his face just enough to portray innocence when a single glance told Meg there was none to have. Roguish scruff along his sharp jawline because that was still in. Startling dark blue eyes that portrayed a quiet cruelty.

Oh, I'm getting all tingly.

She schooled her face into an almost but not quite naïve gaze and rose. "Chris?"

His eyes did a fast tour of her. So fast Meg had no doubt he was unaware he'd even done it. He was sizing her up. Was this one acceptable? Fuckable?

Apparently, she passed, because his face lit up and he moved toward her. Fast for his size, she noted. He took her hand and surprised a laugh out of her by bending to kiss it.

How often had he practiced that very beguiling beta male move?

"You must be the lovely M."

17

Meg nodded.

"And M stands for?"

"Maggie," she lied.

"Wine?"

She hated wine but she could deal with it. "Sure. Pink please."

She had to suppress the urge to roll her eyes. The only thing worse than wine in general was pink wine. But it would please the alpha. And that was the goal. Lull him. Drink with him. Make goo-goo eyes at him. Until it was time.

The thing about predatory men was they hardly ever entertained the thought of predatory women.

SEVEN

MEG

HE DIDN'T NOTICE WHEN SHE put special happy dust in his drink. He was too busy expounding about his daily "brutal" workouts and how his office couldn't live without him. He was a sales rep for a new energy drink.

Of course he was.

He went to flex his biceps and she tipped the powder in and let it dissolve. His beer was stylishly dark and bitter. It would all taste the same.

Meg let him get about half the remaining beer in him and then said, "You want to go back to my place?"

His eyes didn't light up. That would be an expression of delight. Instead, his eyes went dark and narrowed. A hunting animal's gaze. He probably couldn't believe his luck. That she'd go down that easy. Who woulda thunk it.

Not Chris.

"Sure. Sounds fun."

He sounded a little slurred. Not enough that he'd notice. But

19

she did. She had a limited amount of time to get him to the truck before he buckled and it became a problem.

"Let's go."

"Let me just . . ."

Manly man that he was, he grabbed his beer and downed the rest. Again, she had to resist the urge to roll her eyes.

Fine. That's how it was going to be. She'd deal with it. You can't crumble under pressure. It would be stupid and pointless.

Meg stood so he'd mirror her. He stumbled a bit and looked confused.

The bar had picked up. It was standing room only at the moment. Some guys eyed their table as they moved. Chris stumbled again and she heard him mutter, "What the fuck?"

The ones stalking their table, two big bros dressed in Towson University sweatshirts, came swooping in.

"You leaving?" the bigger one said.

This time Meg did roll her eyes and gave a little chuckle. "We are. But he's had . . ." She pointed and shrugged. "I don't know if I can get him to the truck by myself."

She could. But it would be a spectacle. Her dragging his stumbling, sagging ass to the car. She had the muscle, she just didn't want to make a scene.

"Oh, shit. No problem. You parked outside? I can help you."

She smiled. Easy. No man would ever expect a woman to do this. No one would remember it. No one would care.

He put his arm around Chris's waist and said, "Come on, buddy." It was a good natured "bruh" move of epic proportions.

Chris grinned, laughed a little, managed to slur out, "I guess I had more to drink than I thought. She's gonna take me home."

The kid chuckled and started to lead him out. "Sounds good. You're a lucky man. She's a pretty lady."

"Yesh, she ish," Chris said, looking slightly perplexed at his sudden speech impediment.

At her truck, parked in the shadows, thankfully, the kid helped Chris into the passenger seat.

Chris patted him and said, "She's going to take care of me."

Yes, Meg thought, *she* certainly would.

The kid gave her truck a friendly rap on the hood as she drove off.

"Well, that was an adventure, wasn't it?"

She looked over at him. He was asleep.

She patted his thigh.

"Sleep while you can. Cause when you wake up, you're going to wish you were still asleep."

EIGHT

JACK

THE HEADLIGHTS DREW HIS ATTENTION. He was still tidying. She'd been in the house a couple days and she was still a mystery. Casey often stood at the window and watched for her too. Jack imagined it was because Casey wanted to escape him. He was not your average dog owner.

Jack was aware how he came off to others. A weirdo. "Other." He realized it to be true. However, his mother had raised him to be different and embrace it. He'd never been like the other boys, fixated on girls. Always seeking them out, wanting to touch them, wanting to fuck them.

He glanced around the room as if the urn holding his mother's ashes could have heard him think the word "fuck." She did not abide by bad language. Eunice West had been a strict woman who believed in a clean house, a sharp mind, and hard work. She did not, however, believe in God, so when people suggested Jack was a bit different due to a strict religious upbringing, he could only laugh.

He didn't mind that people thought him weird, as long as they kept their distance and minded their own beeswax.

It was his business, and no one else's, that he found a beautiful woman's pain more arousing than a nice body. It was a cleaner connection—more spiritual.

"Spiritual, not religious," he muttered as he headed to the window.

Casey glanced up from his bed, his ears rippling at the sound of Jack's voice. He rose, too, and joined his master at the window.

"Isn't it funny that you're the only being I like to be around for any length of time."

Casey just stood there.

Dogs were perfect. They responded to honesty, no matter what. Unlike women.

The first girlfriend Jack had was twelve-year-old Grace Smith. She'd been as boring as her name. But the thing that drew young Jack to her was her playground shriek. She had a way of hitting a pitch that made most people cringe.

One day, she fell at recess playing soccer. The sounds that came out of her had half the kids in a circle around her. Teachers ran toward her. It was ludicrous, really, that amount of caterwauling for a skinned knee. But for Jack, it had a different effect. He was drawn toward the drama, too, but it was an occurrence he'd mostly ignored until then.

She'd been stunning in that moment. On the ground, bleeding, screaming like a stuck pig. He had to have her.

He asked her the next day to be his girlfriend. He was tired, very tired, he'd been up late into the night thinking about her and that magical pitch she hit with her voice as he did what maturing boys so often do.

Grace had been overjoyed, clearly, until they'd taken a walk in the woods one day. He could tell she wanted him to hold her hand because her pinky kept brushing his as they walked. But he wouldn't. That set his teeth on edge, the idea of holding her germ-riddled, moist hand.

They were deep enough into the woods that he felt safe. He started across a shallow stream, hopping from flat rock to flat rock. And, of course, she followed. He was her boyfriend, after all.

Jack got to the last stone before the other embankment. He turned toward Grace and she beamed, obviously thinking he was going to offer his hand to help her to the end.

Instead, he put his hand flat between her barely there breasts and pushed.

She went down in the shallow water, the bare skin beneath her shorts raking against the rocky bed of the stream. The pain hit and her eyes flared wide and she tilted her average looking face back and shrieked like a woman being burned alive.

He'd watched her, marveling at how the pain turned her plainness into sheer beauty. Jack had absentmindedly fingered the head of his penis as he watched, and when he hit a point where he felt particularly funny, he leaned down and kissed her still screaming mouth.

His pants stained with wetness.

Grace had run home like a hunted rabbit.

When the phone rang later that night, he knew it would be Mrs. Smith. He also knew his mother would handle it. She didn't take anything from anybody. Not ever.

Jack waited there, sitting cross legged on his bed, his knobby knees sticking out from his basketball shorts.

His mother didn't knock when she entered his room. She pushed the door open slowly, though, as if giving him time to get himself together if need be.

"You know who that was," she'd said. It wasn't a question.

He nodded.

"Stay away from that girl, Jack. I told her mother you were just a bit awkward. That the push was an accident and then you didn't know how to react. I told her you were upset, too."

Her eyes, somehow knowing, found his jeans and underwear.

"Put your mess in the laundry," she said softly. "And stay away from girls until you're better at controlling yourself."

He'd taken the note: Not until he was better, or like other boys, but until he handled his urges better.

"Yes, ma'am," he said.

And that had been that.

Jack cut the lights and watched his new neighbor get out of her truck. She had someone with her. The guy looked like a loser, stumbling and weaving. But it was far without the binoculars. Jack couldn't be sure.

She hit the porch and the light flicked on. Her shirt was black to match her hair and her jeans were tight.

His were too, suddenly.

"Dear, neighbor," he said softly. "What do you sound like when you scream?"

NINE

MEG

THIS GUY WAS HEAVY. FUCKING heavy as hell. Getting him in the house nearly took an act of God. Meg worked out daily for reasons just like this, but this guy was like a pillar of stone.

"You'd be very proud of yourself if you knew I thought that about you just now, no doubt," she grunted, sliding him across the living room floor on a rag rug she had rolled up in the closet.

"Work harder, not smarter," she growled.

She got him into the small bathroom off the kitchen and put both his arms up near the base of the toilet. Then she handcuffed one hand to the other. Pulling would get him nowhere. Unless he pulled hard enough to rip the toilet from the wall and tip it over on himself. Then he'd get a concussion.

She smiled down at him. Normally, she'd have done him up in the kitchen on the big table, but she was smart enough to know he was way too cumbersome.

"You're a biggun, Chris. You'd be a real beast if you ever

pudged up."

She nudged him roughly with the toe of her boot. Nothing. He was out.

"That's what happens when you're a big bulky motherfucker. Eating clean and all that. It hits you hard. Worse than a girl," she said, snorting.

He'd be very offended at being likened to a girl.

Meg went into the master bath and took a shower. She turned on only the hot water and stepped inside. It hit her skin like a kiss of fire and only after she hissed did she turn the cold tap a quarter turn to make it a little less dangerous. Touching him had made her feel oily. Greasy. Gross.

She washed her hair and scrubbed her face clean of her mask of makeup.

When she was done, she dried off and put on a pair of comfortable ragged leggings, an oversized sweatshirt that had been her dad's when she was a kid, and cranked the AC. She didn't like the heat. Comfort was the goal.

She poured two fingers of whiskey and then wandered into the kitchen. She stood in the doorway of the half bath and studied her date.

She looked at the tanned expanse of toned abdomen showing above his waistband.

She wanted to cut it. Carve it. Make her mark part of his flesh.

She swigged the drink and poured another. It would be a while before he was awake. He'd had a stronger reaction than she'd expected. She'd read for a bit while she waited for the sleeping princess to stir.

TEN

MEG THEN

*T*HE GIRL WITH NO DADDY.
She hated that they called her that. She hated that they thought it was okay to grab her, chase her, taunt her. The neighborhood was fairly rough. They had to move when her dad died.

Her mother busted ass to make the best of it, and Meg followed suit. She went to school, did her chores, hung at home as much as she could. But her mother didn't understand, didn't get it, and Meg didn't want to tell her. She didn't want to scare her or have her think their home wasn't good enough.

So, when her mom would say, "Go play like a normal kid," she'd put down whatever book she was currently caught up in and pretend to do just that.

Her mother thought she was at Liz's, or maybe even Kara's, but she wasn't. Both friendships had fizzled. The death of a parent matures you. Those girls made her insane, and the bottom line was, they simply didn't get it. So, she pretended to go hang out

28

with them when, in fact, she simply wandered the neighborhood. Sometimes she rode her bike, but often she walked. She'd walk the trench running behind a long group of houses. It wasn't officially a drainage ditch, since it wasn't paved. But the water ran down that way, fast and furious, when heavy rains came. Cut by time and the lay of the land, she liked it down there. Even in the height of summer it was cool. In the winter, if you hit it just right you could sled down it with a nabbed trash can lid or a big piece of cardboard. At least, until it got wet.

She was down there walking when she heard them coming. Tyler, Josh, and Matthew. They hung in a group and were a mere year older than her, but hormones had kicked in and, somehow, while she had grown breasts, they had grown muscles.

She'd been close friends with Matt in grade school, but they weren't in grade school anymore, and he pretended not to remember.

The boisterous forced loudness of their voices sent a cold thread of dread up her spine. She didn't want to come in contact with them.

More than once they'd grabbed her and teased her, Tyler even holding her tight against him once, letting her struggle. Before he let her go, she felt the press of his hardness to her back and had felt a sweeping, staggering sense of relief like no other when he finally released her.

The only place left to go in that particular section was up the right embankment, to the abandoned apartment complex. She'd run around in some of those basement sections with Liz once. They'd even found an old nudie magazine, waterlogged and tattered. Liz had reached for it and Meg had literally smacked her hand away.

"God knows what's on that. Eew!"

She knew more than other girls. About life and about sex. Her mother was an over-sharer, over-prepping Meg for "one day." In this instance, it came in handy.

Liz had rolled her eyes but her cheeks had flamed bright red.

It was that particular unit Meg darted into when she heard them coming. She ducked through the already open doorway just as she heard the biggest one, Tyler, exclaim, "Hey, who was that? Was that little miss Meg, maybe?"

Dread filled her like cold water. She felt her blood draining out of her head. Where it was going, she had no idea. Where did it go when you felt sudden and urgent fear? Wise for twelve or not, she didn't know the answer.

She headed for the steps to take her to the apartment above. At the very least, she could hide there at the top of the steps in the shadows if they came in. When she got closer to the wooden steps, she saw the center section had collapsed. Water damage probably aided by teenagers.

They were coming. She could hear them. Their footsteps, in unison, sounded like soldiers' boots pounding out a tempo on their way to a mission.

She was the mission.

And if they found her, something inside her told her it would be bad. Very bad.

Shadows hovered in the bright sunlight outside the doorway. Them. Coming.

Her heart jumped crazily in her chest, and she thought this was what deer must feel like when people approach.

She'd screwed herself, darting into a building. She'd trapped herself. She headed toward the doorway leading to the next section of basement. Maybe there was a window she could climb out as they were coming in.

No.

It was the laundry area. Three rusted-out washers lay tipped on their sides. The windows were reinforced with chicken wire to prevent break-ins. The dryers were bigger so they were still standing, dented and tagged with spray paint.

"Fuck," she said under her breath. Her hands were shaking, but she did her best to straighten her spine as her eyes scanned the room for a weapon. Anything.

ELEVEN

JACK

HE WAS BUILDING A MODEL. It was one of the things that kept him busy. Before he'd found the model of the WWII Jeep untouched in the back closet, he'd been studying a fascinating book he'd found at the local thrift store. The thrift store was one of his few regular outings. You never knew what you'd find. The heavy tome, published in the 30s, was simply titled *Minor Surgery*. Jack liked to cut things, so he'd snatched it up.

Irony, or maybe fate, made it so the book fell open to the pages for circumcision. Jack had a moment where he considered picking up some men. Circumcision looked interesting.

He knew he was good looking in an unconventional way. Tall and wiry with a shock of dirty blond hair and dark brown eyes. He always called himself skinny, but the men who had hit on him in the past said "lanky" or "lean." He embraced it.

It was flattering to be wanted but men did nothing for him. Looking at the illustration of the simple surgery, he'd thought maybe he was wrong. At least in this case.

Some of the photos excited him, and since he tried to only masturbate once a week at most—for physical well-being—he'd put the book away and found the model. Idle hands were the devil's playground, his mother said. Whatever the hell that meant.

Casey was lying by the front door and he suddenly sat up straight. That made Jack pay attention. Part of why he had Casey was as an early warning system. However, it could just be that Casey was giving him an early warning of a possum or a coyote or a raccoon. All things that Jack didn't care about.

He waited for a few beats and realized he was holding his breath.

Nothing happened, so he returned to his glue and his tiny plastic piece he was trying to put into place with a pair of tweezers.

He was about to set it where it needed to go when someone pounded on the door and he jumped.

"Goddammit," he muttered. It was only when he set the piece down on the desk that he realized what this meant. He had an unexpected visitor after darkness had fallen. Unannounced.

Who?

"Could it be her?" he murmured to himself. The thought that his new neighbor might have shown up to visit him made him shiver all over. It was the closest thing to what other people described as excitement. He only really felt what others told him they felt when he was about to get caught doing something, or getting away with something.

This was neither, really, but closer to the former. Caught doing something. Because if it was her, he'd have to make a split-second decision. Bide his time or react.

Another knock and Casey didn't make a sound. He only banged his tail against the hardwood floor and waited.

"Coming!" Jack called just loud enough to be heard.

He went to the door feeling like he was electrified. It was an adventure, wasn't it, not knowing who was on the other side?

He was both surprised and not surprised when he opened it to find Callie standing there. Leaning. Heavily. Her body seemed propped up by the door jamb.

"Jaaaaaack," she said.

The waft of alcohol hit him in the face. He had to stifle a groan. Drunk. And back. The "back" was the worst part.

"What's up, Cal? Casey has all the food a growing dog would need."

His mother said he was good at camouflaging himself. That he blended in with regular people.

"I want to know why you don't like me."

"I—"

She took a step forward and he instinctively took a step back. Which effectively had her in the house. Damn.

She took her small white finger and dragged it from the neck of his tee to the place where his navel rested beneath. Jack felt a confusing twist in his gut and lower. He both hated her touch and relished it.

"It's not that I don't like you—" he attempted.

"So, you do like me?" She leaned precariously forward and Jack had to raise both hands and grab her upper arms to arrest their movement. Otherwise, they were going to smack faces.

"No, Callie. I don't. I'm sorry." He was losing his patience. That electric feeling had turned to a dull, heavy lead ball in his belly.

"Are you gay?"

He thought of the surgery text, thought of the circumcision illustrations, thought of his interest. He considered telling her yes to get her gone. But then ended up shaking his head.

"Nope. Just not interested in a relationship right now, I guess."

She grinned up at him, still pushing herself against his hands so he had to continue to ward her off. She leaned forward very suddenly and her small hand found its way into his waistband so she was gripping his belt buckle.

"We can just fuck, Jack. We don't have to have a relatible-ship—" She stumbled over the word and then snorted. "Re-lay-shuh-ships—" She enunciated carefully and still messed it up.

"No. You need to go home."

She pressed on, trying to kiss him.

He sighed. He'd lost his manners. He put his big hand over her face and pushed her back. Hard enough to make her stumble, not hard enough to make her fall.

"Jack!" she wailed.

"I said no," he said.

Her eyes narrowed. "What is wrong with you?"

"A lot," he said, laughing.

She came at him so fast he had to react, not think. He clothes-lined her and she went down on her ass on the hardwood. That would have been one thing, but her head snapped sharply against the wall and he watched as she went lights-out. Her big blue eyes rolled back in her head and the room went dead silent.

"Good," he said. "Now I can fucking think."

Casey thumped his tail.

TWELVE

MEG THEN

SHE SAW SOME CHUNKS OF rock and grabbed one. She'd been hoping for a piece of rebar, some broken glass, anything like that. Instead, she found herself in an ugly but not entirely destroyed room that held little that would help her self-defense.

She squatted down and duck-walked behind one of the toppled machines. Its door hung open like a draw bridge. She had a brief moment where she wondered if she'd fit in there. But then she'd be stuck if they found her. At least, behind a machine, she had a chance of dodging them and moving in another direction.

She heard their boots on the concrete floor. Something rumbled, skidded, then clanged. No doubt one of them, in a meager display of testosterone, had kicked something or toppled it over.

Meg wanted to be annoyed. Instead, she was terrified, her heart pounding so hard she felt ill. She always hated being around them. Never liked when they shoved her around or snagged her wrist and held on a beat too long. But this was different. This was dangerous. Every nerve ending in her body sent her that message like a beacon.

She had a very bad feeling that went way down into her bones and she didn't think—not even for a second—that she was over-reacting.

"Who's in here? It's you, isn't it?" Tyler's voice. Deeper than the others, but still cracking sometimes.

She squeezed the rock so hard it cut into her hand and stung. She wondered if she was bleeding but refused to unfurl her hand to check.

Boots clomping, breathing, things rattling as they pawed their way through the room.

Matt saw her first. There was a brief moment of hesitation. When his eyes met hers, he looked like the boy she grew up with. There was a spark of empathy before his expression hardened and he kicked the dryer hard enough to make it rattle and slide slightly across the concrete, exposing part of her.

Her heart fell.

When Tyler came at her, grabbed hold of her, she struck out blindly with her rock. It felt more like a pebble in that moment but it was the only thing she had . . . so she used it. She hit him over and over again and his rage became not just palpable but audible.

He grunted. Snarled "bitch." He hit her so hard her head rang like a bell. She fell back on her left hip against the unforgiving floor, stunned.

Tyler had a red gash on his forehead that bisected his left eye-brow. He had scrapes on his cheek and hands.

Good.

He shook the hand he'd hit her with as if she'd hurt him more than he'd hurt her. Because that's the kind of guy Tyler was.

Matt started toward her and Tyler pointed a finger at him. "Don't. You. Fucking. Dare!" he roared.

Matt froze. He studied her nervously. His expression a mask of worry. This was bad. She was in real trouble.

Josh just stood there like a totem pole.

Tyler yanked her forward and then turned her. He bully-walked her forward until she was face first against the concrete wall.

Josh said, "Hey, Ty, maybe—"

"Shut the fuck up," Tyler snarled. He punched her low down on the small of her back and she sobbed. Her knees sagged, but somehow, she managed not to go down.

Matt did rush forward then. "Let's go. She was scared. She didn't mean to scrape you up so bad. Right?" His eyes leveled with hers and she took the hint.

"Yes. Yes, right," she said through a ragged breath. "I'm sorry," she added for good measure.

Tyler grabbed her long pony tail, yanked her head back, barked in her ear. "You will be, bitch. Trust me on that."

THIRTEEN

MEG

SHE **WOKE WITH A START.** He was floundering around in there. Jerking against his handcuffs. She could hear it. Meg sat up and wiped her forehead, her neck, down into her shirt. Drenched. Cold sweat. Her heart was still pounding and she opened her hand suddenly, sure she'd find a shitty base-ment rock still clutched there.

"It's okay. You're okay. It's fine. You're good . . ." she kept talk-ing until her pulse slowed and she could catch her breath.

"Hey! Bitch!" Chris yelled from the bathroom.

"Shut the fuck up!" she bellowed. Angry. Very angry. Being scared pissed her off and those dreams—that she still hadn't shaken in all these years—enraged her.

"Let me out of here, you cunt!"

Meg shook her head. It never failed to amaze her how the male of the species would talk shit and threaten even when they were undeniably on the bottom. When they were in danger. It just showed how programmed men were to believe they were infallible and invincible. Some more than others.

She climbed off the bed, yanked her sweatshirt off and tossed it on the floor. She found a clean hand towel and wiped herself dry from the residues of the dream. She found a soft cotton tee, so over washed it had holes lacing along the top, and put that on. Soon she'd be cold, but for now she needed to breathe.

"Bitch! Cunt! Whore!"

She shook her head and went in to pour herself another drink. He was a real piece of work, this one. A real piece of shit, too.

She found a thin boning knife in the one kitchen drawer she had fully stocked. She took a long pull on her whiskey and moved toward the roaring voice of an idiot.

She walked into the bathroom where he was sprawled, red-faced, thrashing, utterly angry and baffled.

"You better let me up," he snarled.

"Or what?"

"Or I'll fucking kill you."

She tapped her foot and stared at him. Long enough that his brain made the connection that he was on the floor and she was towering over him.

His tiny mind must have shut down because he went into a frenzy, thrashing and yanking and screaming. "I will, I will fucking snap your neck! You stupid—"

She kicked her foot out fast and pushed it down on his neck. His face immediately became redder and he froze. Wise enough to see he was not in a good situation.

She leaned down, keeping eye contact, and drew the boning knife along his brow, bisecting his left eyebrow. He looked shocked for a second, eyes growing wide, and the blood began to flow and he gave a burbled sputter.

"Listen, cupcake," she said, getting close so he could see and hear her clearly. "Settle down or I will fucking cut your stupid cow throat and call it a night. Capisce?"

Then he understood. Then it sank in. For once, his machismo and gym muscles and intimidation couldn't serve him. For once, a woman was truly greater than him. In a way he could not dismiss.

And it hurt his little feelings.

Meg winked at him and walked away.

FOURTEEN

JACK

HER BOOB WAS STICKING OUT. He tried not to stare at it, but he couldn't help it. Once the caterwauling stopped, the silence was deafening.

He cocked his head, swearing he could hear someone in the distance shouting. Even thinking, for a second, he heard the word "cunt." Which made his head hurt because no one said that word.

He took a step toward Callie and Casey whined.

"Oh, stop. I'm just looking," he muttered.

He liked to think he wasn't a pervert. He'd had sex exactly once and that had been that. While a fireworks display of nerve endings going off and a pleasure that sank down into his bones, the messiness of it didn't appeal to him. Nor did the closeness of it. Even a distant person had to be able to be intimate in, well, a moment of intimacy.

He'd lost his virginity to a girl named Michelle on prom night. An event he'd only attended because it was socially expected of 'normal' people.

They'd had sex in his car. It didn't last long, felt good, and yet, Jack had absolutely no idea what she might have gotten out of it. Given its brevity and his lack of experience, his guess was nothing at all.

But he still found girl bits fascinating.

He inched closer and reached out a hand. Her breasts were small. She rarely wore a bra. This one peeked out at him, the areola a rosy pink fading to pale at the nipple. He reached out a finger and Casey growled.

"Cockblocker," he said to the dog.

The dog put his head down and remained silent.

Jack touched the very tip. Like pushing an elevator button but not as hard.

When her eyes flew open and she started screaming again it threw him off balance. He backpedaled, heart pounding from the rush of sudden adrenaline.

"Fuck!" he said. His ears were ringing.

She jumped up, scrambling, boob still hanging out like some fucking horror movie heroine.

Gotta get the tits and ass in there, Jack thought mildly as he watched her.

She started to run. For the door. And he wasn't sure how he felt about that. Now she had a story. She showed up. He hit her, groped her. He was some kind of sex pervert. How obvious should it have been to them all? He lives up there alone, has weird jobs, hardly ever comes into town, is quiet and reserved. Never see him out dating or attending community things very much.

It all ran through is head like a high-speed ticker tape.

She was clawing at the door like she was in a house of horrors. Which was ironic because she had no idea what that was actually like. If he'd set her out there in his hunting grounds, she'd have every right to be reacting like this, but this . . . this was just fucking stupid.

He tried. He had to. "Callie. Calm down. You were out. I was checking to see if you were oka—"

She turned the lock. The wrong way, he noted. She'd just locked them in.

She hissed her words at him. "You *struck* me. You *touched* me."

He sighed. Suddenly exhausted.

"It isn't what you think."

"Let me out, pervert!" She braced her feet and tugged on the doorknob, practically lying perpendicular to it.

Jack would have found it laughable if he weren't so irritated.

"Callie!" he shouted.

Then she started to whimper and scream again and it was too much. She continued to struggle against a dead bolt she, herself, had locked.

He went to the desk, found the box cutter he used to cut the plastic nubbins off the model pieces before gluing them on.

She didn't even notice. She was tugging and sobbing and fiddling with the deadbolt and she almost had it when he walked up behind her. He grabbed her forehead, wrenched her head back, and slit her throat. More like sawed it, actually. The razor at the very end was pretty gnarly. Time to break that one off and use a fresh one.

He held her for a second before letting her go. She dropped like a bag of stones.

He toed her tit back into her top with his bare foot.

"I'm a killer, not a pervert," he said.

FIFTEEN

MEG THEN

IT HAD LASTED MUCH LONGER than anticipated. She thought boys their age would be done fast. At least that's how she consoled herself as he yanked her shorts down. And then her panties.

She fought. Fought so hard she wrenched her neck and her shoulder and three of her fingers. After, she told her mother she'd fallen in the woods and done that. It explained not only the muscular injuries, but the scrapes and bruises and bloody lip.

Tyler had been first. Of course he had. The big bad ring leader. He'd kept her pressed tight there against the wall. Dust and grit and probably mold filtering into her mouth as she gasped for air. She didn't scream and her crying was silent. She'd had practice tuning things out and pushing them away since her dad died. So many people were cruel. More than you'd expect.

Tyler insisted Josh have a go. Josh looked hesitant. He stepped toward her and tried to turn her to face him. She spit in his face. It was instinct—not a conscious decision—but it was the wrong

45

one.

Anger crowded his features, narrowed his face. He went from a cornfed every-boy football player from anywhere, USA, to a monster.

He pushed her down. Her knees hit the floor, jarred her. He told her to open her mouth.

In her mind, she checked out.

Her dad was there with her. Talking about war documentaries and she was teasing him about how B-O-R-I-N-G they were and why did he make her watch them.

When Josh smashed her flat on her back, his full weight covering her, his breath that smelled like Italian cold cuts and onions invading her nose, it was her and her dad out fishing. He'd always taken her. *Boys, girls, grownups, kids, anyone can fish, Ace.* He'd called her Ace. She didn't know why and, when she asked him, he didn't either.

Then Matt was there. A flicker of hope. A leap in her chest that said maybe here was aid. Help.

He unzipped his pants.

She shut her eyes and went to Christmas three years before when her dad got her that bike she wanted. He thought she still believed in Santa. She didn't. But she believed in her father.

Matt was fast. Maybe that was his mercy, after all.

Meg wasn't sure how long she lay there in the dirt and concrete dust. She slowly became aware of a dull, thudding heartbeat between her legs and the sound of silence. And that meant safety. At least, it did if she got out of there now.

She found her shorts but couldn't find her panties. No matter how long she looked.

She gave up, found one of her sneakers by the door, and only then realized she only had on one. She pushed her hair back and sucked in a breath. Her mouth hurt, her lips burned, her entire body was a giant, throbbing nerve ending.

She limped to the door and peeked outside. They were gone. Birds chirped, something small moved in the brush. She saw in the sky that it was headed toward dusk.

How long had she been there? She began the slow limping journey home.

When she got in, her mother rushed to her. Meg pushed her off, gently. All she wanted was to shower until her skin peeled off.

"It was just a tumble. I wasn't paying attention. I'm fine. But I'm dirty, Ma."

"Are you hungry?"

She wasn't. But she said, "After. I want to shower."

"Okay." Then her mother shook her head. "You really have to be more careful, Meg."

Yes. She did.

SIXTEEN

MEG

SHE FINISHED HER DRINK AND made a sandwich. She hadn't realized how long it had been since she'd eaten until his blood was on the knife. That made her cranky.

She rolled some shaved parmesan and ham into lettuce leaves and gave them each a smear of mayo. She liked to eat low carb when she could.

She inhaled two of them while pouring another drink to calm the electricity raging beneath her skin. When she got a new one, she always had this confusing mix of rage, fear, and excitement. It was like Christmas morning if Santa had left a pit viper in the box.

She wished she still smoked but smoking was bad for you.

She ate the last lettuce roll and took a swig of the new drink. Then she walked forward quietly on her bare feet to check on her guest.

He lay there, clutching his now-coagulated wound. His eyes were wild like a cow going to slaughter. His body rigid. He'd wet his pants.

48

She took the boning knife from her pocket and squatted down over him. His eyes got even bigger. She hadn't thought that possible. She pointed with the very sharp tip.

"What a mess you made, cupcake."

"Why?" he asked, voice harsh and dry.

"'Cause you pissed your pants, obviously."

He shook his head. Anger flitted across his features like a cloud passing in front of the moon. He wanted to insult her, rage at her, yell. He wanted to put her down for her comment. But he was wise enough now—understood her a bit better now—so he stifled it.

Impressive.

"Now, what am I going to do with you?" she asked.

"What *is wrong* with you?" he said, seething. She saw it again—the urge to shout—and waited to see if he'd crack. He didn't.

"Well, let's see, gang rape at twelve. Then I had my hypersexual years . . ." She tapped the boning knife against her lower lip, thinking. "Then I couldn't let anyone touch me. Got funny in my head. Killed a man who tried to hurt me. And then I decided, you know, why get involved with good men and possibly harm them when you can clean up the trash for all the other women out there."

She smiled because his eyes went wide again.

"Yes, you. You are the trash, cupcake."

"Why do you keep calling me that?"

"Why do you call women babe? Honey? Sweetie? Gorgeous?"

He looked away. She waited.

She tapped his thigh with the knife. "That was an actual fucking question, *Chris.*"

He kept his lips pressed together. His eyes averted.

Until she plunged the tip of the boning knife into the meatiest part of his thigh. Making sure to not even get a little bit close to anything that could kill him.

Yet.

GO DOWN HARD

He howled. He sounded like a great wounded beast in the forest.

"Oh, this is nothing. You have no idea. Now answer me."

"I don't know!" he managed. "I just do! I just do it!"

"Don't they have names?"

"Yes!" He was crying now. She liked that. She ran her finger through his tears and rubbed them between her fingertips. They were warm.

"Why don't you use them?"

"I don't know, you b—" He caught himself.

She *tsk*ed. "See, it's always there in you. In guys like you. Just beneath the surface. Like hives that haven't come up yet. It lurks. You think you have the *right* to everything. Money, an easy time at life, whatever toys you want, *women*. We're just another thing you can attain, use, have domain over."

She worked his expensive sneaker off as she talked and he started to thrash. Kicking.

"No, no, no!" Cupcake was possibly the loudest one she'd ever had.

She rose fast, and kicked him hard. He froze, stunned.

"Look, cupcake. You can be still, or I can blindly go at it and it will be worse—much worse—for you. I guarantee it."

His leg thrashed as if of its own accord and then he steadied himself. She took the knife, and while watching his pretty prick face, sliced a red grin into the bottom of his foot. Not too deep. Nothing that would endanger his life but, by fucking God, it would *feel like it*.

He began to howl again and she sighed. She stood and went into the kitchen. She opened the one fully stocked drawer and rummaged. Sometimes she liked to hear them scream, but sometimes it was too fucking loud and it put her nerves on edge.

She found the roll of duct tape. It had small skyscrapers printed all over it. Why go plain silver when you can go fancy?

She ripped off a good section, walked in and slapped it over his gaping mouth. He struggled, bucked, sucked air heartily through his nose.

"Shut up, cupcake. Or I'll do your other foot. Get your shit under control. We're not even close to done for tonight."

She gave him another wink and went back to her drink. The TV was a drone in the background. More bad news from Washington and the White House. More bad news for sane people, like her, who couldn't comprehend what was happening. She watched for a moment before turning away. Seriously, what was the world coming to?

SEVENTEEN

JACK

HE SAT THERE IN THE living room listening to the cicadas screaming in the trees. He drank an ice-cold Coke from the can. Jack didn't drink. He thought it made people messy and stupid. They made poor choices.

Case in point, Callie. He'd had absolutely zero intention of ever hunting her. She wasn't even on his radar. First of all, she was too close. You don't shit where you eat.

That made him think of the girl next door. Next door, obviously, being the next closest house. She was a risk, but she was new and she intrigued him, and sometimes he liked to roll the dice and risk being caught. There was a certain thrill in it, after all.

He looked over at Callie with her artfully arranged top, thanks to him. The ragged hole in her neck had stopped oozing. There was a crust of blood along the edges. Her mouth was open. Her eyes were open. That stuff you see in movies about gently shutting someone's eyes once they've died . . . that's bullshit. Short of glue or heavy coins—or fucking staples—those eyes are staying open.

"You just had to go drinking and come calling," he shouted at her. "And if you'd just played along I'd have let you go."

He sighed.

The dog got up, walked in a circle, then went behind the easy chair in the corner to hide.

"I wouldn't have killed you, you dumb cunt!" he suddenly roared.

He threw the empty aluminum can which held zero satisfaction.

He shook his head.

"And Jesus, I didn't even get to hunt you or play with you or keep you in the cage and make you sing. What a waste." He shook his head in disgust and got off the sofa.

Jack grabbed the can and crumpled it. He put it in the designated recycling can as he went through the doorway between dining room and kitchen. Save the Earth, after all.

He bent to rummage through the stuff under the sink, only to find the box of contractor bags he kept there was shot. Just an empty box.

He thought about throwing that, too, before realizing it would be as futile as the can.

"Jesus . . ." he grumbled.

He tossed the empty box in with the recycling and went down to the basement. There had to be another box down there. He usually bought in bulk. It would probably only take one. Callie was petite. But if he couldn't fit her in one, he could definitely fit her in two. A seal of duct tape where they met and he'd be good to go.

What a waste of a perfectly good woman, he thought.

He went down the steps. At the bottom, he ran one hand lovingly along the bars of the cage. He could, if he shut his eyes, picture her in there. Begging him to let her out. Offering him all kinds of things. Flashing him those tea cup tits of her own accord. Promising him everything from her silence to the use of her body.

He pressed his hand against his fly. In his mind, her screams echoed, and he took a brief moment to take care of his predicament and then clean up after himself.

At least something good had come from it. He felt a bit more relaxed.

Then he spotted the box of bags on the shelf over the workbench and smiled. Things were looking up a little bit.

He'd been collecting screams for years. Some of them were even on tape. Some only on digital. Some only in his mind. Once he'd videotaped a girl while he played with her. His mother had found it and pulled it from the VHS casing right in front of him. She'd tossed it in the kitchen sink and set a match to it while simultaneously flipping the switch for the exhaust fan.

"Jack, I thought you were smarter than that. This is evidence. This could get you in big trouble. Everything you need to hold onto, you need to hold onto in here." She rapped his temple hard with two fingertips.

It made a dull thump-thump sound deep inside his head.

Then she'd taken a long wooden spoon she used for dumplings and ravioli and beat his ass black and blue with it.

He was fourteen.

Bigger than her.

He took it.

"I think," he said to Callie as he bent her small body to see if it would fit into one contractor bag, "that my mother was collecting my screams. Maybe my father's before me. He left us, you know?"

He looked down at her with her clean, fresh looks, her pale bleached hair, her big blue, now-glazed eyes, her small breasts, and her look of surprise and said, "I don't know if he left us though. Something tells me she got rid of him. Just a hunch."

His mother's paramours often "stopped coming around" but bits of them were still evident. A money clip here, a razor there. A lock of hair on her dresser. Once he'd found a gold tooth.

He shrugged.

Lots of unsuspecting people over the years had looked at him and his mother and said, "Like mother like son." Jack thought that might be more accurate than anyone suspected.

He stood back, *tsk*ing. "I don't think you'll fit in one. I have to find the duct tape so the animals don't get curious before I can bury or dump you."

He left her there, upper half spilling out of the bag like the worst-case scenario of Santa's sack ever.

EIGHTEEN

MEG

SHE POURED ANOTHER DRINK BUT only took a sip because it was hitting her. A bit too hard, perhaps. She wanted to be on top of things. No fun having fun if you were too shitfaced to have fun.

She popped her head in the bathroom. "Hey, cupcake, you smoke?"

His eyes narrowed despite his palpable fear. He shook his head. Probably best for him that his mouth was taped because she thought if his mouth was operable he'd have said something he'd have regretted.

She walked in and sat on the toilet lid, legs spread, looking down at him. He was upside down to her but still his fear and anger warred clearly on his face.

"You know . . . I looked you up. 'On the line,' as my former landlady would have said. After you messaged me. You used your whole name. Which is kind of fucking stupid, cupcake. But you're proud of who you are, aren't you? Even though you probably shouldn't be."

He was watching her the way campers watch an unexpected black bear approaching camp. Which was wise of him.

"I found not one . . . not two . . . but three mentions of rape and assault charges brought against you."

His wary eyes flared wide. The fear was back.

"And yet, you got away with every one of them. Daddy settling for two, and it seems, I mean . . . I can only theorize, you or someone close to you, scaring the other poor girl. It all went away, didn't it?" She kicked his shoulder. Hard.

He grunted, flailed, tried to work his way across the old linoleum floor to get away from her. But there was no getting away from her. He knew it and soon he'd accept it.

She got up slowly, feeling that whiskey. Wishing she had a cigarette. She took a deep breath and squatted next to him. The boning knife was in her belt loop. She pulled it out. Showed it to him.

He started flopping around again like a fish on a dock. He tried to go left, he tried to go right, but the bottom line was Chris the predator could only go a few inches in either direction.

She worked his other shoe off and he started to scream but it was muffled by the tape. She'd heard a scared horse screaming once. That's what he sounded like.

"See, the thing is, you got off with, what those of us who've been . . ." She petered off, tapped the knife against her chin, thinking. "I don't want to say *victims*. I hate that word. Let's say, those of us who've had encounters with men like you. That's better. Anyway, it's what those of us who've had encounters with men like you call the 'boys will be boys' defense."

He stared up at her. Eyes leaking tears. Nostrils flaring with every breath he dragged violently inward. He was in full-blown panic and it was gorgeous.

"I'm here to rectify that," she said.

"No-no-no—" But it came out "oh-oh-oh" from beneath the tape.

"Oh, yes," she said. "See, I like to find guys like you and turn the tables. I like to make the world a safer place for my less experienced, more naïve sisters who haven't been hurt by men like you. I'd like to keep them that way if I can."

She opened up the bottom of his left foot with a single swift cut.

He screamed behind the tape. He tossed. He muttered things she was sure were threats and some she guessed were promises and a few that might have been pathetic efforts at apology.

"I like to be their guardian angel," she said. "Because Christ knows I never had one."

Once he stopped all his noise, she stood and went back to the kitchen. She found the derringer in the kitchen drawer, two shots, just enough to do a swift job. She made sure she had two more sets of cuffs and that the big-ass table was clear of debris. Then she went back.

"I can't get to you the way I'd like down here, cupcake. We're going to move into the kitchen." She waved the gun so close to his face his eyes crossed. "And you're going to behave because I don't want to have to shoot you in the dick. Ya hear?"

He nodded. He was on board. He would behave.

"Good." She leaned forward to undo the cuffs and got slightly lightheaded. She knew better. One drink max when she had company. The dreams, though. They always made her want more. To drown them out.

She got the cuff to pop. Her foot fully on his chest until she stood. Then she aimed the gun at him and said, "Get up slow or you'll be down a ball. Maybe two." She aimed the gun at his crotch to make sure he understood she wasn't fucking around.

He came up slowly. Stood with his hands in the air like she was a cop. And shambled as best he could on two bloody feet just a few steps ahead of her.

Then she caught an elbow to the face and the world shook. She started to go down, caught herself on the table, and watched him hobbling toward the back door. She aimed, fired once, knowing she hit something because he yelped.

"Fuck!" she growled.

But then the asshole was out the door and running like a mad man. She took off after him, thankful they were in the sticks. Thankful no one around here knew her.

He lurched across the yard toward the road and somehow put on speed.

She put on speed herself. Sweating. Cursing. She had no one but herself—and whiskey—to blame.

NINETEEN

MEG

SHE ALMOST CAUGHT UP WITH him but tripped over a rock. And now that he was up and running, all of his apparent gym haunting was coming in handy. Why couldn't she have a guy who loved pumping iron but shunned cardio? Not her luck, this guy was like a terrified jackrabbit now that he'd hit open ground.

"I will shoot your ass," she shouted.

She tried to line up a shot but he started zigging and zagging. Probably shouldn't have announced that.

She shut one eye but with the lack of depth perception coupled with whiskey, that proved to be a bad plan. She stumbled and barely caught herself. And since the gun had no safety, she felt damn lucky she hadn't shot herself.

"Jesus fucking Christ . . ."

She panted and huffed and put on speed. She was barefoot like him but he was scared and she was just annoyed. Meg felt every pebble, every divot, every stick. She'd kill him quick now just because she was pissed.

He veered uphill from the main road and she suddenly realized what he was doing. He was headed for the house. The one where her friendly neighborhood binocular snooper lived.

The lights of his house glowed like a beacon through the trees. The cicadas screamed. She hissed. Considered throwing the gun at his fucking head to see if that would work.

He just kept running. The lights drawing him like a moth to a porch light.

She was about a hundred paces behind him, trying desperately to put on speed and catch up. If he went in that house she'd have to kill him *and* the binocular owner.

No doubt.

And she didn't want to shit where she ate. She just got here.

He went down with a thud and a cry. She thought she'd get lucky and catch up with him. Put a bullet through his head and drag him home. The shot wouldn't be too terribly loud from a little gun. It would sound more like a car backfiring.

Unfortunately, Cupcake had some serious motivation and sprang back up like an extra in a Bruce Lee movie. He was back on his feet and bolting before she'd even closed half the gap.

"Fuck!" she grunted and kept running. She stumbled, bit her tongue hard, and the rage that flowed through her was apocalyptic.

When she caught him, she was going to pull his skin off in strips. Feed them to him. And cut his throat one fucking inch at a time so he could get the full experience. Screw a bullet, she'd make him suffer slowly.

She crested the hill in time to see him hit the front porch running. It was a big painted wooden number and his bare feet beat a heavy tattoo across it as he ran.

She hesitated and shrugged. It was the time to run away or go all in. Meg put on speed. She was right behind him.

Cupcake lucked out because, apparently, the door was unlocked. He turned the knob, fumbling for a moment, and then burst through. She heard him call, "Hello? Help! Hello?" before he'd fully cleared the threshold.

Adrenaline had given her speed. She was right on his heels.

She raised the gun and found the weirdest tableaux.

Cupcake huffing, puffing, bleeding, staring at the freshly killed body of a young blond woman. The girl's lower half was tucked into a giant black garbage bag. Her upper half lolled against the wall, her throat black and red with a ragged wound.

The man standing in the adjoining room was handsome in a skinny rock star way. He looked amused. Not afraid.

Cupcake looked confused. He finally said, "Help?"

Then she walked up, put the gun to the back of his head, and fired.

He went down like the sack of shit he was.

The man in the next room said, "Hi?"

And she just started to laugh.

TWENTY

JACK

HE WASN'T SURE WHAT TO do. Which was unusual. Very little flustered Jack. But he had to admit, he had not been expecting a bloody man to fly through his front door, followed by the woman who appeared to be his mysterious new neighbor, and then for her to murder said bloody man.

She laughed for a moment longer, holding her stomach. Then she bent, hands on thighs, trying to catch her breath.

She looked up at him, eyes wild. Jack felt the tightening in his pants. When it came unexpectedly it usually irritated him. This time, not so much.

"Hi," she said. "Have any whiskey?"

"I don't drink," he said.

For some reason, that made her laugh harder.

Jack studied her. Her hair was dark like crow feathers. Her eyes were dark too—shiny with laughter. The whites were impossibly white. They almost seemed to glow.

She shoved the tiny gun in her front pocket. She had her phone in the other pocket and it was actually larger than the pistol.

"Got any more of those bags?"

He looked where her gaze had gone. The contractor bag half covered Callie like a giant plastic snake eating its prey.

"Yeah."

"Can I have one?" She cocked her head. "Two. Maybe even three. Got a saw or should I get my own?"

He was already moving. Going toward the kitchen where the bags were.

"Why cut him up? You can just dump him way back on that property of yours. The animals will find him."

She ran a hand through her hair, making it stand on end. It reminded him of a mohawk. She had a very warrior feel about her. Tribal. Dangerous.

His stomach tumbled like he was falling.

He pressed his palm low on his gut but that only made it worse so he stopped.

She'd followed him into the kitchen. She hovered there in the doorway like a dark wraith, watching him move.

"I have a saw if you really want one. But—"

"I can't drag him back there alone," she said. "I guess I could get my truck."

He found it interesting she had yet to mention Callie. It wasn't every day a man had a woman in a bag inside his front door. Then again, it wasn't every day a woman chased a man inside a stranger's house and then shot him at point blank range.

"I can drive you back. I have a Jeep. We can drive him up into the hills and dump him."

She seemed to consider the offer. "What about Miss Trash Bag USA over here? What are you going to do about her?"

"I had intended to bag her up and dump her later. But I guess we could get them both up in the hills and leave them."

"In for a penny, in for a pound," she said.

He opened the fridge and handed her a Coke. "Closest I have to booze."

"It's not even in the same county," she said. "But I'll take it."

She cracked it and guzzled half the can in about three swallows. Then she belched.

She stuck her bloody hand out. "Meg," she said.

He realized how much he was attracted to her. Lustful, even. And alternately, how badly he still wanted to kill her.

He took her hand and shook. "Jack." Then he smirked and said, "That's Callie in there. She surprised me tonight."

Meg cocked an eyebrow. "Guess I got off lucky then."

"You *really* surprised me." Jack surprised himself by giving a genuine laugh.

"Well, I assure you that wasn't planned. That was all him."

"And he is?"

"Oh, him? That's Cupcake," she said, then snorted. "My date for tonight."

"Much more than just a run of the mill black widow," Jack joked.

"Honey, you have no idea." She finished the Coke and crushed the can. She tossed it his way.

He barely managed to snag it out of the air. Then he dropped it in the recycling and went to get the keys to the Jeep.

He wasn't sure why Michelle had suddenly popped into his mind as he dragged Cupcake, or whatever his real name was, to the Jeep. They'd swapped. Meg was behind him, grunting as she dragged the bag full of Callie toward the vehicle.

She was strong, he noted. Biceps stood out in sharp relief in the cold white moonlight. She stood, rubbed her palms on the ass of her jeans, then bent back to the task.

His dick was hard. He was thinking of Michelle. Only, he didn't think it was Michelle, actually. Jack was fairly certain he was recalling the long-ago *act*. One, it was dawning on him, he thought he might want to perform with Meg.

Watching her calmly shoot this man in the head and then ask for a drink had done something to him. Woken up something inside him no other woman had managed to stir to life.

It was weird.

It was distracting.

He wasn't sure he liked it.

But one part of him was certainly on board.

He dumped the guy in the open back of the Jeep. He'd removed the rear seat ages ago. It stood out, rusting, in the old barn.

He moved to grab Callie from her and she snapped, "I've got it. I've got it!"

He shook his head and stepped back. Watching her muscle Callie up into the Jeep and the way she ran both hands through her hair again, clearly not worried if she messed it up, only punctuated his attraction.

"Why my side of the road?" she asked.

He couldn't see her. Just her outline as she was backlit by the glow from his house and the moon. But he could imagine those dark eyes of hers boring into his core. Seeing inside him. Knowing him.

He cleared his throat and brought his brain back on track.

"More hills on that property. More critters who will venture down. Bigger ones. If you follow my property back far enough it hits the highway. So . . ."

She gave a succinct nod. "Right. Okay." She raised one foot and stared at the bare sole. Then did the other. "Asshole," she muttered. "Tore my feet up."

He smiled in the dark. She felt the same way about the guy she'd shot as he did about Callie. It was their fault. And they'd caused inconvenience.

They climbed into the Jeep. The doors were off. The top was

off. It was just the frame.

"So, you like watching me from across the road, eh?" She put her bare feet on the dashboard. He didn't say anything.

"I was curious," he said finally. "The house has been empty a long time."

She nodded.

It was lighter now that he was traveling down toward the road. It lit her up. Pretty face, hair like some crazy bird, perfect sized tits—as if he believed in such a thing—leggings leaving no mystery to her curves.

Dirty feet.

The feet should bother him. They didn't. She'd earned them chasing Cupcake. And she'd won.

"What are we going to do now, Jack? I know your secret. You know mine."

He stopped at the foot of his driveway. The light from the moon and the streetlights lit her up now.

"I don't know."

She stared at him. "She wasn't your first, was she?"

He didn't hesitate. "No." He watched her for a beat. "He wasn't yours, was he?"

"Fuck no," she said.

He nodded and hit the gas. Interesting.

TWENTY-ONE

JACK

HE WENT WELL UP INTO the hills.

"Is this my property?" she asked.

"I have no idea."

Meg laughed. "Who cares. As long as no one sees us, we'll be fine."

In a clearing inside a copse of trees, they dumped them. Jack literally opened the tailgate door on the Jeep and they rolled the bodies out. They stripped them of the plastic bags. Those they'd take home and burn.

Funny, she'd gone from not knowing her neighbors to committing a crime with one. It goes to show, you just never know.

They finally climbed back into the Jeep and Jack turned it around in a wide semi-circle, going downhill now. The hard terrain of the hills was bumpy. The tires kicked up dust even in the darkness. She found herself laughing because it felt very much like the vehicle had run away, propelling itself downhill at a breakneck speed that might kill them both.

It was amazing.

At her house, he stopped.

It was a strange not-date date moment. She considered asking him in for a drink.

Instead she asked, "Have you ever had sex?"

He didn't look surprised. She doubted anything surprised him. He grinned and it turned her on and scared her a little at the same time. An unusual sensation for her. She had mixed feelings about it.

"Once."

She nodded. Not surprised. "Once was all you needed."

He seemed to consider his words. "I thought so."

Curious, she thought.

"You want to come in for a drink?"

"I don't drink, remember."

"I have things besides booze, you know."

He nodded slowly. "I believe you. But I should get back. Clean up some."

Meg snorted. "Me too."

He was looking at the top of her thigh. She doubted he realized how obvious it was. "You want to touch me, don't you?"

He looked up at her. This time there was a spark of surprise in his pretty, dead eyes. "Yes. I do. I'm not sure why."

"Because I'm like you," she said. "And you didn't really think that was possible."

She took his hand and put it up high on her thigh. So the tip of his pinkie brushed her in the spot he was curious about.

He squeezed. Then he squeezed harder. A sparkle of pain flared along her thigh and she felt it go straight between her legs.

She was starting to have unclean thoughts about Jack.

"I think we should have dinner," he said.

"Out?" she asked, a bit surprised.

He grinned, shook his head. How could anyone look at him and not see a killer, she wondered. It was so obvious.

"I'll cook," he said.

"Okay. Meat," she said.

"What?"

"I like meat. I don't do the whole vegetarian or vegan thing. No meat, no dinner."

"How's steak?"

"Cooked how?"

"Medium?"

"Perfect," she said.

She moved his hand very briefly up to cover the V between her legs. Just thin cotton leggings between his hand and her bare body. She saw a beat of surprise and something darker lurking in his eyes.

Then she moved it, dropped it in his own lap, and got out of the car.

"It was nice meeting you, Jack," she said.

She walked inside before he could answer.

Meg poured herself a whiskey. The exact thing that had gotten her into this mess. But she knew the whole flirting—if that's what you could even call it—thing would bring the dreams.

The dreams were the only thing she really feared. Getting caught, she didn't fear. Getting hurt didn't scare her. One of these men besting her didn't even create a worry crease on her brow.

But the dreams, she loathed those. When they came, they came hard and fast like an overflowing river in storm season. They swept her down and under and tossed her about. She'd wake, heart pounding, old internal scar tissue aching, hands pressed into tight fists—so tight it was hard for her to unclench them. She'd wake crying or, worse, screaming.

She hated it. That feeling of vulnerability she always felt when she woke from one of the nightmares. She'd take any physical pain, any emotional abuse, any mental torture over feeling vulnerable. There was no greater indignity, in her humble opinion. And she had suffered her share of indignity.

She swallowed the amber liquid down in one knock, hoping against hope it would keep them at bay or drown them out entirely.

She doubted it, but she could hope.

"Should have asked Dexter up there if he smoked." Then she snorted. "If he doesn't drink, it's doubtful he smokes. Killing is his drug." She wandered to bed, dropped on the mattress. "I can dig it."

And she could.

She'd clean up in the morning. Then she'd decide about Jack. She kind of wanted to fuck him . . . but she kind of wanted to kill him, too.

TWENTY-TWO

MEG THEN

SHE'D NEVER SEEN SO MUCH blood that wasn't from her period. Every time she peed, it stung. Every time she sat down, she winced. Her knees were black and blue the next morning. Same with her lip and jaw. She tried to cover some scratches and bruises on her forehead with her bangs but they weren't long enough.

"I told Mrs. Stevens about your tumble. She said you're too much of a tomboy." Her mother chuckled as if this was the funniest thing ever.

This wouldn't have happened if you hadn't sent me out there. If you'd have just let me read . . .

But her mother didn't know what had happened so the words died inside her mouth—bitter on her tongue. Her mother was doing what mothers do. Patrolling, policing, encouraging—*forcing.*

Plus, Meg knew damn well it could have still happened. Those boys, they'd been out for her for a while. She'd just thought it bullying, but what had happened had happened way too fluidly to be spur of the moment. At the very least, Tyler had had it in his head. He'd been the leader of the whole thing.

She picked at her sandwich. She'd lost weight in just a few days. And she tried to remember when her last period had been because she needed to watch for the next one.

The only thing more infuriating than what they'd done to her would be something coming of it. Something she'd have to take care of. Alone and in secret. She wouldn't even know where to begin. Rachel at school had an older sister who sometimes picked her up after the bell. She could ask her. She might know. The older girl smoked and wore a lot of makeup and had a boyfriend who drove a Camaro. It was the only person that came to mind. The only person who maybe wouldn't tell.

Her mother was staring at her.

"Oh, yeah. I guess. But better to be a tomboy than a princess," she said because it's the kind of thing her mom would expect her to say.

Her mother rolled her eyes and put some dishes in the dishwasher.

She wondered if that part of you could scar. She was pretty sure—as she shifted again—that it could. They'd torn her. And taken something from her that was supposed to be hers to give.

Tears shimmered along her lower lids. She could see them turning the bright sunshine coming in from the kitchen window into prisms. She blinked repeatedly, swallowed convulsively. When her mother's back was turned, she grabbed her napkin and wiped them furiously.

She could cry later. Her mom was just starting to be more like her old self lately. She'd been very down and very removed since Meg's dad died. This would kill her. There was no way she was going to tell her mother. Which meant there was no way she would tell *anyone*.

Unless something came of this.

GO DOWN HARD

She thought she had only three more days to wait and see. She was fairly regular.

But three days was going to seem like forever.

She managed to avoid them at school for the most part. The only one she crossed paths with regularly was Matt and he couldn't—*wouldn't*—look at her.

She wanted to scream at him the most. Pervert! Rapist! Abuser!

Once upon a time friend.

She teared up every time she saw him.

The stinging when she peed was starting to get better, but her period still hadn't come and she was trying very hard not to obsess. Sometimes she was a little late. A little late was okay.

On the way to school one morning, her mother dropped a bomb that shook her fragile mental state. Meg's hands started shaking the moment her mother informed her. She was driving, fiddling with the radio when she said, "Oh, I forgot. I have a doctor's appointment at 3:30, I won't be able to pick you up so I need you to walk. It's a nice day, though, right?"

Meg could only nod. All her words had flown away. Her fear was a beast imprisoned in her chest. It was living in a cage too small and flexing its wings.

She picked at the knee of her jeans.

"I'll make it up to you," her mother said, sensing something was off. "How about burgers for dinner? I'll get you fast food. That's how sorry I am!"

Meg tried very hard to smile. "Great," she said.

When her mother let her out of the car, she saw a piece of glass—thick green bottle glass—by the curb. It had a wicked curve that gleamed in the sunlight.

She took her tennis shoe and kicked it beneath the bush closest to the stone bench in front of the school.

For later.

TWENTY-THREE

MEG

SHE WOKE AT THREE-THIRTY because she had to pee. No dreams she could recall. That was good. That was unheard of.

She went to the kitchen, stood there thinking. No dreams. She poured herself a big slug of whiskey to try and keep it that way.

She was drinking too much lately. She had to do better.

TWENTY-FOUR

JACK

JACK LAY THERE FOR WHAT felt like forever. His dick went in and out of hardness. He refused to touch it. Even through every memory of her bursting in like some woodland warrior with dirty feet and sticks in her short, choppy hair made him want to. Every remembrance of the gun shot—how it had rattled his bones.

He didn't touch it because it somehow felt like a commitment. An admission.

Plus, he'd already had his taste earlier at the cage. Can't be greedy.

Masturbation was messy and sometimes tedious and always conjured the voice of his mother in his head. He sometimes used it as a sleeping aid or stress relief. Medicinal purposes, if you will. But tried not to.

He was a man and he knew how the human body worked. He also knew sexual outlet was normal, healthy, and, in some respects, good for you. It didn't mean he needed to like it.

In this instance, it was worse than the nastiness of need or the urges of the common man. It felt like a submission to unexpected attraction. Jack was unaccustomed to that.

There was an intimacy in the disposing of the bodies that hadn't escaped him. Her request for a saw had been stunningly sensual, he had to admit. And the lack of fear of him—well, he didn't quite know what to do with that.

He wanted to bed her. It was a term his mother had used when she was alive. He found it more palatable than the other options.

He also wanted to hunt her. Put her in his little cage. Make her scream. Break her. Then set her loose and stalk her.

Jack thought she'd be an amazing hunt. Fierce and not easy in the least. She'd fight tooth and nail, fist and elbow, until the bitter end, he had no doubt.

He smiled in the dark when he realized he was assuming he'd win. That he'd best Meg.

His mother had taught him lessons about what can happen when you assume.

The sun was peeking above the tree line when Jack finally drifted off to sleep. Outside, the cicadas screamed.

TWENTY-FIVE

MEG

SHE WOKE UP PUNCHING. SCRATCHING. Kicking. She came up out of the dream as if surfacing from the depths of a cold, dark lake. It took forever. Things were murky. Greenish around the edges. Her limbs weighed down with phantom lead. Her head pounding like a rotten tooth.

"Fuck," she snarled. She put her hand to her forehead like she could stifle the pain. It felt as if her brain was trying to escape.

She rolled to her side, a slight wave of nausea overtaking her. Then she inhaled deeply and pushed herself into a sitting position.

Her bladder throbbed and her mouth was whatever lay beyond dry.

She coughed, coughed again. Then rubbed her forehead hard and fast. So hard the skin burned beneath her fingers. It was a trick a guy she'd dated briefly used to do if she had a headache. Supposedly, it brought blood flow to the area and helped get rid of pain.

In reality, she had no fucking clue why it worked.

She groaned and got to her feet. She stood there for a moment to get her bearings. Bright shards of sunlight burst through the sheers.

"I need actual fucking curtains," she informed the bedroom.

In the bathroom, her pale face greeted her in the ancient age-speckled mirror. Her hair stood up in crazy spikes and whorls. She turned on the tap and filled her cupped hands with water. First, she drank a slug of it. Then she splashed it on her face. She shrieked at the coldness, but did it again anyway.

Served her right. Fucking up like that. Being so sloppy. Letting him get away. If Cupcake hadn't had the most colossal bad luck she'd ever seen, stumbling into the home of an entirely different killer, she'd have had a busy night.

She'd have had to kill him and the innocent bystander.

Turned out, the bystander wasn't so innocent.

"You fell ass backwards into that," she told the woman in the mirror. "That could have been bad bad bad."

It wasn't the torture and the blood and the murder that made her want to drink when she brought a guy home. It was the possibility of the dreams. The killing was supposed to help the dreams. Sometimes, it didn't work. Sometimes, it only made her feel better in the moment.

Meg didn't think anything would ever truly make her feel better. At least this had a reason. It served a purpose. She was cleaning up for other girls. Other women.

She turned the shower on as hot as she could and let it steam up. It was going to be a warm one outside but she needed to sweat out some of this booze. The last thing she needed was to smell like her mother years after her dad's death.

Meg's mom had hung in there until about the seven-year mark. Then sadness and not being able to find a decent man did her in. She'd started an optimistic campaign to find a suitor about three years after Meg's father's death. It had been a stunning failure.

GO DOWN HARD

Each guy she brought home was worse than the last. And her mother knew it, too. It hit her hard. She was of the generation who thought, without a man, a woman was an old maid. Useless, worthless, and unlovable.

Meanwhile, Meg was going through boys the way she went through tissues when she had the flu. Each one was a victory. Woo them, fuck them, dump them—remaining in control and keeping them at arm's length the whole time.

Nothing made her dump a guy faster than him saying he had feelings for her.

She could remember coming home from dates, to find her mother chain smoking, watching *The X-Files*, and drinking Johnny Walker Black. She'd be able to smell her mother's breath from the front door, before she even approached her.

She'd want to hug Meg. Brush her hair back. Talk about her "date." Was he a nice boy? (He's decent in bed). Was he a gentleman? (He made sure I came first.) Was he funny? (He thinks so.) Will you see him again? (Depends on my craving for sex.) Can I meet him? (A resounding no.)

Meg stepped into the shower and the water seared her. She let it pound down on her.

It was in those moments—where her mother was fully plastered—that Meg hated her most. That she blamed her the most. That she wanted to take the sickness and the darkness and the rage living in her head since that long-ago day and smear it all over her mother's rosy, drunken litany of questions.

Instead, she'd mutter her answers and escape. She knew it was in honor of her father that she didn't spill all that internal poison all over her mother. He'd loved them both. They'd both lost him. It wasn't worth it. She knew, in some way, she'd always think he'd be disappointed in her if she did that to her mom, and that was unbearable.

Her father's memory was the only truly pure, untainted thing in Meg's life. She wouldn't piss all over it for a moment of relief.

She washed her hair and tried to breathe. She'd drink a bucket of coffee, a vat of water, eat some buttered toast, and clean up.

There would be dried blood and footprints and other kinds of shit from her fuck up to deal with.

Memories that somehow, miraculously, didn't encroach on her sleep, tried to slip into her mind as she stood there. She pushed them away by bending and turning the hot water knob farther. Her skin sang, begging for mercy.

Meg ignored it.

She scrubbed the blood up with disinfectant wipes. She could do the whole bucket and mop thing but why? She'd only just gotten started. Granted, it took nearly a whole canister of them to clean up, but whatever. She scrubbed the old grimy tile well, filled a plastic grocery bag with the rust-colored wipes. She even cleaned the toilet inside and out, just in case.

In the kitchen, she found the whisky bottle. It's green glass barely managed to shield her from the fact that most of the amber liquid was depleted.

She groaned aloud, grabbed the bottle, and stood on tiptoe to put it in the cabinet above the sink. She lost her grip on it and it toppled, bouncing off the lip of the sink, shattering on the way down.

She froze, floor littered with shards of broken glass. She was barefoot. Not in the mood for an emergency room trip.

She squatted down and got another grocery sack from under the sink. She started to put the most wickedly sharp bits in the bag. One thick chunk caught her attention. She picked it up. Sliding her finger along its deadly curve. Not hard enough to cut herself.

She heard something. Then realized she was sobbing.

TWENTY-SIX

MEG THEN

THEY WERE TRAILING HER. **THEY** had been all day. Every time she rounded a corner and was alone for a moment, her heart beat so hard she felt sick with it.

They had stayed a few feet back, like a pack of hunting hyenas, but Meg knew they were there. They'd flare out and walk three-wide. Then contract into a single file line. All the while joking and laughing loudly.

She stepped outside into the sunlight and looked around hopefully. Maybe her mother's doctor appointment had been canceled. Maybe she had finished early. No such luck. Her mother's baby blue sedan was nowhere in sight.

She lingered by the school because it made her feel safer. Close to the building. To teachers and other students and some form of contact. The boys caught on and hovered on the periphery, near the entrance, horsing around, acting like any other boys in the world.

Meg stared longingly at the sidewalk leading to the main road.

She just wanted to go home. She wanted to lock herself inside, find something stupid on TV—a talk show maybe—and read. And pretend the terrible trio didn't exist and most certainly didn't mean anything to her.

No one outside but them. The majority of kids had already gone—been picked up, hopped a bus, or walked. The teachers remaining were inside grading papers. The students remaining were inside at extracurriculars.

She glanced down to see the piece of green glass she'd stashed beneath the bush. She'd forgotten about it somehow. The day had been busy and when she wasn't near the three of them her brain liked school. She liked to think and learn and she certainly liked a challenge.

"Maybe she's ready for round two," Tyler crowed, boldly. No one to hear him but her. He didn't use her name. He could easily claim it as an allusion to something totally unrelated.

The front door swung open and her heart leapt. It was only a kid, much younger than them, even. No help.

The kid spared a curious if not annoyed glance at the three loud boys and then went on, backpack nearly bending him in half as he walked.

She took advantage of the distraction to stoop down and stash the green glass in her pocket. She fingered the tip. A razor-sharp curve. The rest of it somehow not very sharp—like beach glass.

None of that mattered. It was something. She couldn't just stand here all damn day and hope they lost interest. And a part of Meg absolutely refused to be their victim. What had happened was over and she wouldn't live under the cloud of fear or their bullying. She absolutely would not.

She'd rather be dead.

She shouldered her own backpack, putting it on properly instead of just slinging it over one shoulder like she normally would. This would make her balanced and she'd be able to use both hands.

GO DOWN HARD

Should she need to.

God, she didn't want to need to.

She started to walk. Meg didn't look back but she heard them slouching after her. The scuff of sneakers on macadam and the lazy way teenage boys walked.

Her stomach rolled sickly. Her head buzzed a little. She kept walking. Spine straight. Head up. Eyes wide. Fingers grasped around the chunk of glass in her skirt pocket.

What they didn't know could save her.

She was fine walking the sidewalks from the main building to the main road. She walked with confidence despite a pounding heart and knees that felt made of jelly.

It was fine when she reached the main road. A busy intersection, four-way stop, kids still lingering as they walked home without rush. There was the crowded bus stop with not just kids who lived farther away than the school bus would take them, but adults coming or going to work.

She hoped beyond hope—it was a ridiculous hope, she knew—they'd lose interest and leave her alone.

But all the while she could hear them. Snickering, joking, tossing out ballsy statements like "hot to trot," "can't forget about me," and "raring to go."

She thought she might vomit. Every punctuation of Tyler's big dumb voice followed by the slippery sniggers of the other two flooded her head with the smell of that basement room, the taste of concrete dust gritty in her mouth, hunting for her panties.

She squeezed the glass until she felt a small puncture and then the slick feeling of blood in her hand.

She was fine until she wasn't fine.

There was a stretch of woods on either side of the street she had to go down. A good block of no houses, little traffic, and few pedestrians.

And that is where they got her.

TWENTY-SEVEN

JACK

JACK WOKE HIMSELF BY JERKING off furiously.

It had only happened once before. When he was about fourteen. He'd woken simply going to town and on the razor-sharp edge of orgasm.

He'd heard his mother's steps on the hardwood floor in the hall. Already up and moving around. Early to rise and get the day started.

And yet, he'd been so close, he couldn't stop. Even with the threat of her throwing open the door to greet him with horror.

He'd simply kept going. Hearing the toilet flush. Hearing the water running. And then knowing she was stepping out of her long pink robe and letting her smooth dark hair out of the cage of its clip.

His ejaculation had been so sudden he'd sobbed aloud.

He heard the door to the bathroom creak as if maybe she'd heard him and was coming to check.

He hurriedly found a sock on the floor, cleaned himself up,

turned it inside out. But she hadn't come to inspect.

This time he was right there again. His hand a blur on his erection. In his mind, it wasn't his mother—it was her. Meg. Her with that gleam in her eye. Her with a saw blade to his neck as she rode him. Her on top—my god, how else would it be with a woman like her?

He kept his eyes clamped shut so he could see it all in his head. The saw changed to a gun. The gun—small and smelling of metal and oil—pressed to his forehead. Then a knife—wicked and long—to his gut. And then just her—no weapons but her hands—as she dug her fingernails into the wells of his eyes.

This orgasm was as violent as the one long ago.

And again, he found a sock on the floor, used it to clean himself, and turned it inside out even though no one would find it. It was just him.

They needed to have dinner.

Soon.

He needed to figure himself out.

Figure her out.

TWENTY-EIGHT

MEG THEN

SHE COULD SEE THEIR SHADOWS approaching. Her heart felt like a frantic creature.

She put on some speed but didn't run. Somehow, she knew running would only excite them. Like wolves or bears. Welcoming a chase would be unwise.

Her hand never left her pocket, that chunk of glass a talisman, a magical item.

She kept her head up, her spine tight, and walked.

She heard his footfalls, clunky and loud, and knew he was coming. It would be Tyler. No doubt. The ringleader. The worst of the bunch.

He caught her around the waist. His reach long enough that the backpack sandwiched between them didn't hinder him.

"Where you going, Meggie? Slow down a little. Spend some time with us."

She struggled, pushing her body forward, planting her feet, tilting away from him in an attempt to break his grip.

He responded by jerking her up and off her feet before letting her slam back down as if to say, *You can do that, but look what I can do.*

Bigger.

Stronger.

Men—boys—usually had the upper hand.

Unless you had a weapon.

His grip slackened a bit and she made an attempt to run. Put on some speed. Yes, it would entice them but if she was fast enough and could clear the sections of trees, she could start shouting at the houses—any houses—for help.

He thundered behind her and snagged her by the backpack. He pulled her off balance, nearly jerking her off her feet.

Meg screamed. Still in the trees but it didn't matter. She screamed because she was scared, she screamed because not again, hell no not again, she screamed because she was angry.

He yanked her once more, laughing, and she turned her body, moving into the thrust, the chunk of glass cutting into her even as she did it—but she didn't care.

It hit his thigh and she put her weight behind it. Even as it opened her palm like a magic zipper. She plunged the wicked tip into his leg as far as she could.

He howled. Howled like some great wounded beast. Howled like Meg had when they'd attacked her, when she couldn't keep herself silent anymore.

She spun fully to face him, her anger greater than her fear in that moment.

Matt looked up at her, bleeding.

Matt, not Tyler.

The other two boys hung back, eyes wide, unsure.

Good.

She ground out each word like she was spitting out coins. "I will tell. If you ever touch me again, I will tell. Every single one of you. I will go to your parents. I will tell them. I will tell school and the police and anyone who will listen. I will tell them until they listen."

She reached forward and Matt actually flinched. Good. She ate that flinch like the finest meal. It filled her. Satiated her.

She tugged the glass out slowly. Bit by bit as he lay there mesmerized.

She pointed it at each of them just as an oncoming car started its way through the false dusk created by the close-set trees.

"Touch me again and I'll fucking kill you. See if I won't," she said. Then she jabbed the glass back into the meat of his thigh, got up, and walked away.

She kept waiting. Waiting to get in trouble. Waiting for someone to come. Waiting.

No one ever came.

No trouble ever came.

The boys gave her a wide berth after that.

She'd wake up dreaming of the feeling of the resistance of flesh and muscle and sinew against a chunk of thick green glass. Those dreams she liked.

TWENTY-NINE

JACK

SOCIOPATH.
    Psychopath.
    Personality disorder.
Depression coupled with high anxiety.
Bipolar.
Jack had heard them all. But no one had ever narrowed it down. There had been a point where he'd tried. Well, more accurately, tried to try. Tried to want to fit in. To care. Tried to figure out who he was—what he was—and figure out if he could be a normal person.

The more he tried, the more bored he grew. If all that monotony was what being 'normal' was, no thank you.

Nothing got his blood going like bringing a pretty girl home, letting her think he'd prepared her a lovely romantic dinner, and then locking her in his cage.

When he shut his eyes and inhaled deeply, holding that breath and letting his heart beat hard, he could call up the sound of the last one's cries. She'd been a beauty. Long blond hair, big blue eyes, small breasts and a trim waist. She'd made him want things.

But more than those things he wanted the symphony of her cries. Wanted to hear her terror.

She'd screamed, cried, begged, and bargained.

He'd sat at the top of the basement steps and listened. Ate it up.

When she finally fell asleep, he crept down and watched her. Watched her toss and turn. Watched her shallow, rapid, fearful breath, even in slumber.

Jack had quietly unlatched the door to the cage. She'd stirred but not woken. Then he tiptoed back upstairs, knowing that if—when—she woke and made a break for it, his little rigged alarm would alert him.

He'd fallen asleep with a hard on. Very aware his whole body was partially straining, listening, waiting for that alarm.

It had come at about three a.m.

He'd shoved his feet into shoes. It was warm and the gym shorts he slept in would be just fine for a chase. He tugged on a tee, pocketed his phone, and took off after her.

She was at the top of the hill when he burst out of the kitchen door. She saw the flare of light. Heard his pounding footfalls. She'd looked back, squawked like some temperamental parrot, and tried to put on speed.

Poor thing, Jack thought. No shoes. Cold. Tired.

He grinned in the dark. He could feel it stretching his face. It wasn't real joy or even amusement. He didn't process those things like others. This was thrill. This was blood lust. This was the sheer and utter rush of adrenaline and blood while he hunted.

Hunted the beautiful, the coveted, the unattainable.

Tara—her name had been Tara—had cried out. Convinced, somewhere in her mind, she would be a final girl. She'd be the girl in the movies who survived. Who cut down the serial killer. She'd be the one who prevailed.

Jack laughed. He heard the lunatic lilt of it as he galloped after her.

"No! No!" she kept yelling as she ran, stumbled, righted herself, ran again. She kept chanting it at him over her shoulder like it would stop him. As if that single word of denial was a weapon against the force of his need.

Jack had news for her . . . it wasn't.

She'd run into the car barn. He'd hoped she would. He burst in a minute after her. He surveyed the automotive graveyard the barn housed.

He held his breath, trying to still his pounding heart. Listening. Listening for her.

There was a rustle. Just a small one. His eyes strayed toward the white, rusted-out '66 Mustang and the shell of a very old, authentic Army Jeep. He took a step in that direction. He sidled. He danced. He made his way toward those humped shapes and, as he got close enough to the Mustang, she cried out, shrieking. He went in one side as she tried to snake out the other. He snagged her ankle, pulled her toward him.

She kicked at him but, skinny or not, Jack knew how to fend off a blow. If you were going to be the kind of hunter he was, you had to.

He caught the foot she directed at him and held onto the heel. Squeezed. Tipped her toes back toward her body. Stretching, pushing, forcing those muscles and ligaments.

Her wide eyes went wider. Her cries hit a pitch that was a heavenly chorus to his ears. He kept pushing, forcing, until he felt something ping. *Ping!* Like a rubber band snapping.

His money was on her Achilles tendon.

She screamed, throat raw, chest heaving. Then he shoved her whole body so she slid out the opposite side of the back seat and hit the filthy barn floor with an audible thud.

"You have five seconds to get moving," he said softly. But he knew she heard. "Five . . . four . . . three . . ."

He heard her scrambling, gasping for air, sniffling, and wheezing. But the most beautiful sound of all was the sound of her dragging that foot. Hauling that wound around.

The barn door suddenly burst open and showed the dark mottled night sky. The moon had gone behind some clouds.

Jack took a deep breath, blew it out, chuckled with satisfaction, and took off after her.

He touched the lock of her hair and looked toward the house. Meg's house. Now he knew it was Meg's house.

He saw nothing. No movement.

He brought the binoculars up and trained them on the front windows. She had sheers up. Now that he'd met her, he'd wager those were the ones that came with the house. New curtains and a home makeover didn't seem her thing.

The one window—kitchen maybe—showed movement beyond the sheers. But that was all he could make out. Just the flicker of motion in the shadows of the room.

He glanced at the blood in the foyer. Some from Callie, a good portion from the man she called Cupcake.

The gun had been too small to blow any real mess around. It just sort of scrambled his brains inside his head for the most part. Good. That was good.

Jack knew she'd gotten lucky. Often a shot from such a small caliber could stop a man but not kill him. At least not right away. She hit something spot on because he'd gone down instantly.

She should look into a bigger gun.

He stared longer at the spot. He should clean it up.

He peeked out the window again. The sheers were still closed. He detected no movement beyond.

Jack went to the kitchen, filled a bucket with ammonia and

water. His mother said nothing cleaned like it. Jack always answered, "Nothing *smells* like it, that's for sure!"

She'd laugh and he'd feel proud.

She used a lot of ammonia to clean. Over the years, Jack wondered if there was a reason for that.

He added some very hot water and mixed it with a mop and went to town in the foyer.

He thought about her bursting in the night before. Dark eyes wide and predatory. Chest heaving. So pretty. So dangerous. And so glib.

He normally didn't like glib women. They were offensive to him somehow.

He started to scrub.

"More mess from her than me," he grunted as he really worked a blood spot.

"She owes me one."

THIRTY

MEG

SHE'D BEEN FISHING PIECES OF glass out from under the kitchen table. Where was her fucking vacuum cleaner when she needed it?

She froze when there was a knock at the door. She put the thick sickle of glass into the pocket of her shorts.

Meg sat back on her haunches and stared at the kitchen door. Beyond the white curtain that covered the window of the door was the dark outline of a person.

Mailman? Avon lady? Jehovah's Witness?

"Jack," she said under her breath.

She climbed to her feet and pushed the broom in front of her as she walked to the door.

She peeked around the edge of the curtain to be certain before flinging the door open and inviting a stranger—as if he wasn't a stranger—into her home where blood and evidence still lurked.

Not that she thought anyone in a million years would think her guilty of anything other than flirting with men and liking whiskey.

Oh, how naïve.

It was him.

She unlocked the door, twisted the knob, and pulled it open. "What's up?"

"You owe me," he said.

Amusement and annoyance flowed through her in equal measure.

"Do I now?"

He took a step toward her, paused, gauged her reaction, then entered the kitchen. Despite the fact that it was sunny outside, her kitchen was gloomy. The sun wouldn't reach this room until just before it went down.

"I just cleaned up my mess *and yours*," Jack said. A coy smile, or sinister, she couldn't tell yet.

"Is that right?" She swept her arm toward the kitchen, signs of Cupcake making a break for it and her clumsiness still evident.

"You should have waited. I could have come there once I finished here."

His eyes were pale blue with the slightest mesmerizing green ring around the pupil. They looked so charming and harmless. Not the eyes of a man who'd have a woman half in a bag in his foyer.

He shrugged. "It's fine. I like cleaning. But I think that dinner should be tonight."

She leaned her hip against the kitchen table and shifted her weight. She felt a shard of glass bite into her foot, the prick of blood, but didn't let it show.

"Do you want to woo me, fuck me, or kill me, Jack?"

He studied her long enough, in silence, that she wondered if he would speak at all.

He said, "I'm still trying to figure that out."

Meg chuckled. "At least you're honest." She raised her foot, looked at the bright crimson dot of blood. Jack did too.

"Be a good boy and fetch me my flip flops from the bedroom. I made a mess in here by accident."

When he turned to do her bidding, she patted the glass in her pocket. It made her feel better that it was there.

He returned and handed them over, his cool eyes studying the floor and her long legs. She felt aroused and wary at the same time. Which was the perfect way to sum up being the recipient of male attention.

She dropped the shoes, slid her feet into them, ignoring the grind of a bit of glass in her foot. Then began sweeping.

Jack spotted the dust pan in the corner by the trash and retrieved it.

When he pressed it flat to the ground in front of her, she swept her collected glass into it.

"Look at us," she said. "Two killers working together."

He grunted, a small smile playing across his lips. "How did this happen? Did he do it?"

"He pulled everything down and made a mess. I dropped a whiskey bottle and that's where the glass came from."

He regarded her with a straight face. "That's why I don't drink," he said, voice low.

"You don't drink because it could hinder your control. And you like to control everything. Your environment, your thoughts, germs, dirt, your victims, your dick."

Two bright spots appeared on his cheeks. She smiled. She'd hit a nerve. He didn't drink and he didn't like that he had a libido. But at the same time, he did.

THIRTY-ONE

JACK

WHAT DID HE WANT? HE wasn't sure. He turned it over in his mind as he helped her sweep up the glass. Then he pointed to the chair. "Sit."

She eyed him warily. "Why?"

"Let me see that foot. Even a tiny piece of glass can get you a nice infection. Trust me, I know infections." He grinned.

"Well, a germaphobe would."

"Borderline germaphobe," he said. "But close enough."

She shook her head. "Borderline, my ass."

But she dropped into the kitchen chair and put her leg up so her calf rested on the table and her foot was in the air. He took off her flip-flop and dropped it.

"Your feet are still filthy," he said.

"I *was* chasing Cupcake barefoot through the dirt and mud and grass and up the fucking road. I showered this morning, don't worry."

"I'm not worried," Jack said. "Do you have a first aid kit or do

I have to go get mine?"

"Under the sink," she said. "Alcohol, bandages, ointment, and all that jazz."

He retrieved it and did a quick scan of underneath. Household chemicals, the stuff she mentioned, clothesline, clothespins, razor wire. He shut the cabinet. She had a little goody kit under there.

He nodded, giving her foot a clinical probing. She winced when he hit the spot where the minuscule bit of glass had lodged itself. How could something that small hurt so much?

Jack swabbed her foot with alcohol. She didn't really react beyond saying, "Cold!" He pushed where the small red dot was and she winced again.

"I'm going to probably dig around a little in the meat to get it," he said.

"I'm sure that breaks your heart."

He chuckled. She was funny. Her wit was biting—borderline cruel—and reminded him of his mother somewhat.

"It's killing me," he said dryly.

He continued to swab her foot until it looked relatively clean. He couldn't bear it otherwise. Then he squeezed the flesh around the tiny puncture.

She hissed between her teeth. "How can something so little hurt that fucking bad?"

"I was just wondering that myself," he said.

He poked her with the tweezers and she remained stoic. So, he poked her harder, plucking at the skin to try and extract the tiny bit of green glass.

"I can feel it grinding," she said almost conversationally.

He nodded. Poked, plucked, felt it catch, lost it.

"Dammit," he said. "I had it."

"Try again." She wiggled her toes. He let her finish and then went back to it. He caught it again, just the tip, felt the glass grind against the tweezers, then felt it slip away.

"Shit."

"You know, if you're thinking of having me to dinner and trying to kill me, you should know something."

She said it as if she were telling him the weather forecast. She wiggled her toes again.

"What's that?"

"Women like me might go down . . ."

He caught that it was a double entendre. That she was deliberately provoking discomfort in him.

"But?"

"But we go down hard," she said. "If your plan is to try anything with me, it won't be as easy as you think. Certainly not as easy as I'm sure it's been for you in the past."

"I would imagine so," he said, focusing on that little glimmer of green in her foot. He caught it, held it, pulled it free.

Success.

"So, you might want to decide if you want me to be your friend, your lover, or your victim real soon. Because two of those are probably doable. One is not."

She wiggled her toes again and he watched her. He had the wild thought to raise her foot, stick her big toe in his mouth, suck it.

He dropped her foot, not sure what to do with the direction his brain had just gone.

She laughed softly, curled her leg under her and looked up at him.

"So, what's for dinner?"

"Apparently," Jack said, "you require meat."

THIRTY-TWO

MEG

SHE WATCHED HIM WALK BACK up to his house. He had the easy loping stride of a cowboy or a surfer. He kind of went at his own pace without any awareness of his angular body.

She patted her pocket again. She'd have to make sure she had the glass. Or more. Best to be prepared when dining with Jack.

Meg wasn't sure which excited her more. The idea of maybe sleeping with him or the danger of knowing he might try to make her a victim.

It had been a long while since she thought of herself as a victim. And the challenge of fending off that possibility while being aware that it was something he might be planning was intoxicating.

"You're fucking nuts, woman," she said to herself.

She remembered his dog. Why did he have a dog? Most people like him hurt animals.

"Probably to look normal," she said. "And maybe for instances like this, Meg. He can talk to the dog and not himself."

She got on her hands and knees and did touch-ups with the wipes. Then she logged onto her work account and checked in. She did freelance editing and wrote for some magazines regularly. She was crazy but she was also a hard worker.

A lot of her dates showed up with wads of cash to impress, so that often supplemented her indie income. The house down payment had come from her mother's death benefits.

Cirrhosis of the liver. Yeah, big shock.

She answered one of her clients, checked her bank balance, and looked at the messages she'd gotten from her dating app.

Cupcake had been a bust. She'd have to find someone else who caught her fancy.

There was this guy. Todd. A big ruddy guy with a buzz cut. Bright blue eyes and a smug look. He was the kind of guy who was big and buff at the moment but eventually would pork up, no doubt. You could tell by the shape of his face and neck.

"Poor baby."

"Hi there! I wanted to say hi. You're very pretty. I'd love to take you out for a drink. I'm looking for a special lady."

Meg rolled her eyes. "Special lady" was basically a generic term for getting laid. Preferably right away.

Just like Cupcake he'd used his full name. She set about to googling.

Looking at him didn't spark any wariness in her, though. But you never know.

A quick search of him and his area offered up absolutely nothing on Todd Smyth. Nothing. Not long ago or recently.

She swiped away from him.

"Sorry, man. Not my type."

The next message was her type. A dark-haired, dark-eyed, tall man. First name: Michael. Last name: Flay. He had a record of attempted assault on a female student from the sister school of his former Catholic high school. Charges had 'later been dropped' which meant the archdiocese had taken care of their boy. The girl had moved to another state.

His second set of charges came from a college party. A girl claimed he'd drugged her and had sex with her while she was unconscious. Michael Flay claimed she'd been drunk and had come on to him and that the sex was consensual. Shockingly (not really), he had more witnesses than her and he was given a slap on the wrist and a warning to be more careful.

Because girls, you know, can be so dangerous.

"I can," Meg whispered.

She read his message—typical hi, I'm so and so and work at such and such. Then she answered him, smiling the whole time.

"Not sure of my schedule yet but I think soon I can take you up on that drink if you're still interested."

It didn't take him long to say yes.

"Great!" she typed. "It's a date! I'll be in touch."

First Jack. And if she survived that, she'd tackle Michael Flay. Possibly literally.

THIRTY-THREE

JACK

HE'D HAVE TO GO INTO town. It occurred to him someone might ask him about Callie. It had also occurred to him her car wasn't out there. Had she been dropped off? Used a car service app?

"I have no idea," he said aloud to practice. "Last I saw her she dropped off Casey's dog food. I was supposed to come in and pay. Which is why I'm here."

He shrugged. Sounded good to him. He'd go in and pay for the food and see if anyone bothered to ask him.

He took his phone—normally abandoned on the kitchen counter—and made a short list.

Ribeyes, baby red potatoes, fresh corn, some sort of store-bought cake. Whiskey for her? Maybe. That should do. Simple. After all, besides the dinner part, he had no idea what would happen. Her having whiskey and him being a teetotaler might work in his favor.

He got his earth friendly reusable bags and clicked his tongue

104

for Casey, who diligently followed his master out to the Jeep.

Jack got in and Casey jumped into the passenger seat. Jack gave him a cursory pet. "Good boy. You're good for my image, you know."

Casey sighed as if he totally understood. He couldn't contain his glee, though, once the ride started. He was a dog, after all.

Town looked normal. Too many people on Main Street. Going about their lives, butting into each other's, gossiping, and watching one another. He avoided town for a reason.

When he went looking for a date, he went way north in the state or down into the city. Often, he'd hop across the border into Pennsylvania. In dive bars, people rarely asked questions. They were focused on their booze and their own shot at getting laid.

However, Jack was smart enough to know that avoiding town *too* much would make people talk. He had to walk a fine line. He felt he did fairly well.

He patted Casey's head, knowing lots of eyes were watching. "I was due to come in anyway, boy. I guess I'll live. We'll go to the feed store first."

Good Grub fed every animal in town from hamsters, gold fish, all the way up to bulls. It was a big place and animals were welcome as long as they were well behaved.

"Come on," he said and whistled.

Casey jumped down and together they went into the cavernous store, Casey stopping every few feet to sniff the sawdust on the ground.

Jack went to the counter, already reaching for his wallet.

Blake, one of two regular counter workers, saw him and gave him a nod. "Be right there."

"No rush."

Casey came to Jack and sat by his feet.

He looked down at him. "Go on and look around. Explore."

The dog seemed to shrug and got up to make the sniffing

rounds.

"What can I do for you?" Blake said, wiping his hands on a rag.

"I came in to pay for that food Callie dropped off."

Blake rolled his eyes and said, *flake* under his breath. To Jack, he said, "Let me pull up your account."

Jack waited as he ticked two fingers on the keyboard.

"One bag, right?"

"Yep. So far. If I like it—well, if Casey does—I can call you guys and put together a bigger order."

Blake nodded. "You betcha."

"It's 39.99 a bag. With tax . . ."

Jack didn't wait for him to finish, he handed over a fifty.

"Great," Blake said, then made change.

He handed back the change. Jack realized that Blake wasn't going to ask about Callie. There was a deflating feeling in his chest. The absence of the thrill of being challenged.

He smiled. "Where is Callie, anyway?" he asked. As if he didn't know she was dead and rotting in the hills behind Meg's property. "I wanted to thank her for dropping that bag off to me. She didn't have to do that."

Blake rolled his eyes. "She's not here. She missed her shift. We called her but no answer. It's not the first time."

"Ah," Jack said.

"You haven't seen her, have you?" Blake asked, pretty much an afterthought.

"Not since she dropped the food off. But if I do, I'll tell her to call in."

"She'll be lucky if she still has a job," Blake said. "Tom doesn't like slackers."

Jack nodded. "Understandable. Thanks much, Blake. I'll see you next time."

He gave a low whistle for Casey who instantly materialized like a ghost in a haunted house. He patted the dog and out they went.

Now he'd go to the grocery store. Get in, get out. That was the plan. Being amongst the unwashed masses always set his teeth on edge. Unless he was looking for one in particular.

A flash of blond hair caught his attention and his mind went right back to his last chase.

She'd hit the ground running, so to speak. Out the barn door, darting up the hill. Darting was a strong word. More like hopping.

Jack had to give her credit. She'd stopped to grab a big stick and was using it as a walking cane. Helping to drag herself uphill.

He hung back a little, just to give her hope. Whatever he'd done to her ankle had slowed her down significantly, but she wasn't ready to surrender.

"Here I come!" he yelled like a war cry.

Her sob echoed down the hill. Then "No!" A beat or two and a breathless "Please!"

Jack chuckled and took off after her. He crested the hill and looked around. He didn't see her. And there was no way in hell she'd gone down the other side that fast. He stopped, held his breath, listened. The noise of crickets and cicadas and then, under it, barely audible, but there, her soft breathing. She was trying to stay quiet.

He followed it. Making sure he didn't give himself away with noise. Until he was close, that was. When he was close to her, he stepped on a twig, deliberately.

So she would hear the sound. Feel his presence.

The soft breathing turned into a mewling sound.

That went right to the man part of him. That sound. It was music to his ears.

She was inside an overgrown bush. It formed a barrier around her. He could just make out the glint of her white skin in a slice of moonlight.

She had her head buried under her arm, it looked like, but he wasn't entirely sure. It was too dark to make out one shadow from another.

When he was up close on the bush, he squatted down quietly, listening to her whimper and moan.

She had her hands over her head. She was hiding inside the cage of branches and her own arms.

"Boo!" he said, and shook the branches.

She screamed. Her voice a silver thing darting around and batting against the night sky. Trapped.

He chuckled, thrust a hand into the bush, grabbed her hair and yanked. He yanked her toward him, not yielding to any of her struggles.

He pulled her out and stared down at her as he continued to hold her long hair. He wrapped it around his fist, getting a closer hold. A more painful hold for her.

"No-no-no-no-no . . ." A moan and then more of her mantra. "No-no-no-no . . ."

"Did you really think you'd get away from me?"

"I'll do anything," she said. "Anything you want. Take my clothes off. Take *me*," she said. "I won't tell."

He punched her in the face then. Stunning her into silence. In the darkness and mirror of moonlight the blood fleeing her nostrils looked black.

"Shut up. You should never barter yourself to anyone. Ever."

She looked more stunned at his statement than from the blow.

"But I—I will. I mean, I won't tell. Isn't that what this is all about?"

Sex. She thought it was about sex.

Jack shook his head. Stupid. So stupid.

This time, what he bent and bent and bent until he felt a *ping* was her neck. Only it wasn't so much a ping as a crunch. A very deep satisfying snap like a thick dry twig.

"That's what this was about," Jack said, and let her slide down from his grip.

The moon seemed to surge—cold white light illuminating her pretty pink lips.

Jack bent down and touched them . . .

He pulled into the grocery store feeling a little flushed and short of breath. Remembering always did that.

He had to sit in the driver's seat for a moment before he could get up and go. He looked at Casey. "Stay," he said.

Casey seemed to nod. Casey wouldn't move. Casey knew better.

THIRTY-FOUR

JACK

THE GROCERY STORE WAS ALWAYS too busy for him. The old ladies who wanted to talk, the workers who wanted to guide you to whatever products they'd been instructed to push, managers who got up in your face wanting to know if you were finding everything okay.

Jack did his best to glide by all of them with minimal interaction. The only people he ever felt any kinship with were the surly bag boys who looked like they just wanted to make it through their shifts so they could get the fuck out.

He grabbed two very nice, thick, well-marbled ribeyes and made his way down toward the produce section.

He fondled handfuls of small red potatoes until he had about a dozen. He stroked some local corn until he found four perfect ears.

An old woman watched him, her face fixed in distaste. Her mouth puckered like a hot pink-painted asshole.

Jack winked at her.

She shuddered, glanced at the ground, moved along.

He couldn't suppress a chuckle.

He often wondered if some people picked up a certain vibe from him. He'd heard, more than once, of people who had an inkling that a person was a killer. Or "off." They sometimes led to that person's arrest.

Jack liked to think himself brave and unflinching but he wondered, at times, if he avoided town so diligently because he feared this happening to him.

The old crone with her beady eyes and her over attention to him was somewhat unsettling. He didn't feel fear per se, at least he didn't think he did, but he felt wary at times.

People like that made him wary.

He passed a display of sparkling cider and that brought up the whole booze thing again.

"No whiskey," he said under his breath as he approached the cake display. "Even playing field."

If she was going to lose to him, it would be because he had bested her, not because she was inebriated.

If that were to happen.

He shook his head. As if that weren't going to happen. The question wasn't would he try to kill her. The question was, would he try to bed her first.

And something told Jack that Meg was thinking the exact same way.

This pleased him.

He managed to make small talk and check out without too much more scrutiny from nosey octogenarians.

THIRTY-FIVE

MEG

SHE'D READ HER FAIR SHARE about women "like her." She knew there were various reactions. Some women never recovered—never craved sex again. Couldn't stand to be touched. Some women became hypersexual. Some women could only bare the gentlest of lovers, some women only the roughest.

Don had been a lover who had, at least in the beginning, given her what she wanted. Pulled her hair, spanked her ass, hickies, bite marks (don't break the skin, please and thank you). A hand to the throat occasionally. Plenty of sex, plenty of orgasms, plenty of endorphins.

Then he'd lost his job. Had trouble finding a new one.

And one night while fucking her, he'd grabbed her neck and squeezed. At first it worked for her. She liked it. Felt herself growing close to orgasm.

Then his grip tightened and her breath was a shallow whistling thing.

She gasped, clawed at him, but his face—so unlike his normal face—enraged and sleep deprived and depressed, glared down at her.

A well-placed knee to the groin brought him down. He'd been her first. Without thinking, she rolled to his bedside table, grabbed an enormous marble ashtray and slammed it into his head.

Her heart pounding, her body still aroused, she wasn't sure if he was dead. She reached into his nightstand where he kept his hunting knives and proceeded to slit his throat.

He'd shown her how once, during normal conversation.

"I said stop," she whispered.

She made sure to wipe down the knife and the ashtray. But she left everything else. She was a regular here. People knew her. Neighbors had seen her. But that night, no one had. They'd come in late. She'd wait and see what happened.

She quickly showered, wiped down the tub and shower door, got dressed and left. She had to walk home because he'd picked her up. But that was okay. It cleared her head.

The police had questioned her briefly. She'd told them they were a thing—mostly friends with benefits—and he saw other women regularly. All true.

They never came back again.

A thrill had slowly built inside her. A thrill that she'd bested him, saved herself, taken his life, and gotten away with it.

Would he have kept squeezing? She had no idea. But she also had no intention of being helpless again. He'd caught her off guard because she trusted him.

He was the first she killed, the last she trusted.

She fretted over an outfit for dinner with Jack. She settled on faded jeans, Vans, a dark purple tank top. No bra. That would throw him.

She jumped up and down, making sure she had good range of

movement. She'd take a sweater tied around her waist in case it got chilly when the sun went down.

Her phone went in her back pocket. The talon of glass—wrapped in a handkerchief—went in the front. The rest of it was up to her.

No gun. Guns were messy and often inaccurate. She knew the one shot she used on Cupcake killing him was a fucking miracle.

As it got closer, their date, she realized she was more interested in a battle than a fuck.

But who said you couldn't have both?

She heard a low rumble and looked out the window. Jack's Jeep went trundling up the main road toward his driveway. She could see his dog riding shotgun.

He'd gone off to find meat. She smiled.

How very domestic. A serial killer shopping for a nice simple meal. Welcoming his neighbor. A reaper of her own kind. She liked to think of herself as a guardian of unsuspecting potential victims.

Taking Jack out wouldn't just be fun. It would be a good service provided to the women who'd yet to meet up with the likes of him.

It was practically her sworn duty to have dinner with him.

She stroked the curve of the wrapped glass in her front pocket. She shut her eyes, remembering, feeling, even hearing the phantom sound of that long-ago glass thudding and chunking into that boy's thigh. She could remember his screams.

Her nipples went hard.

Maybe she should throw Jack off a little. Put his guard up.

THIRTY-SIX

JACK

HE SWORE, AS HE APPROACHED his driveway, he could feel her eyes tracking him. The Jeep rocked and bumped along. Casey sat as patiently as ever. A sentinel to his master's activities.

The back of his neck prickled as if he were in the woods being watched by a wild animal.

Meg was a wild animal and he'd do best to remember that. This was not one of those scenarios where he was going to taunt and play with an unsuspecting innocent woman.

He was going to be dining, among other things, with a woman who had burst into his house in her bare feet with her hair wild and her eyes wide, assessed him and Callie's corpse, and then shot her former captive in the head with casual ease.

Not unsuspecting.

Not innocent.

A feeling he couldn't describe as anything other than excitement unfurled deep inside him as he ripped open the plastic covering the ribeyes to let them rest on the counter and come to room temperature.

"Plus, it gives me an excuse to make an actual proper dinner," he informed Casey.

Casey, who could smell those steaks, thumped his tail against the floor and drooled ever so slightly.

"I'll make sure you get a piece," Jack said. He wasn't a monster.

He took his time scrubbing the potatoes. It was a zen activity for him. Then did the same with the corn, slowly and efficiently shucking each ear and clearing every bit of silk. He hated getting that stuff stuck in his teeth, but loved the sweetness of fresh local corn in season.

This would beat his normal frozen meal or pizza. He really should cook more often. After all, he wasn't getting any younger. Had to stay fast and on his toes.

Time slipped away as he prepped and when someone knocked at the door, he looked up to see it was going on three-thirty in the afternoon. He'd planned dinner for four.

Before he could go in and answer it, he heard the front door swing wide. He grabbed a paring knife off the counter and walked to the doorway.

She stood there. Lean and ready in faded jeans and a tank. Her crazy cockatoo hair stood up in peaks and horns. He was fascinated by it. Along with her big brown eyes and the mole just below the left one. Her face bare of makeup, he didn't think he'd ever seen a more stunning woman.

"Just wanted to pop in and ask what time," she said. She leaned her hip against the armoire in the foyer. She stared pointedly at the place Callie had rested and the spot where Cupcake had gone down.

She smiled. "Nice."

He nodded. Then cleared his throat. Few people could stun him into silence. She could.

"I was thinking four, but I got lost in the preparation. Four-thirty?"

She nodded, smirked at him. Her lips, naturally, were the color of faded prom roses.

"One more question, Jack."

He slid the paring knife into his back pocket then shoved his hands in his front pockets. Relaxed his stance.

"What's your question?"

He stared into those deep brown eyes and waited.

"I don't have to worry about you poisoning me, do I?"

It caught him so off guard he laughed out loud. "No."

She cocked an eyebrow. A talent he appreciated.

"Why the laughter?"

"There's no sportsmanship in poison. It's sneaky and under-handed."

"You've never doped a girl to get her to your lair?"

"Have you ever doped a guy?"

"You betcha. Cupcake, for example."

"Did you do anything to him when he was out?"

"Nope." She shook her head.

"Same here. Drugging might be necessary at first, but is never in the actual encounter. They're awake. Lucid. Able to think and react. Plus, you're coming to my *lair* willingly," he said with a smirk.

"And utterly aware of what you are," she reminded him.

"Back at you," he said.

She grinned. "Touché." She turned on her sneakers. "Back in an hour. Wear something pretty for me." Then she was out the door in a blink.

Jack shook his head. Returned to his potatoes. Sooner or later, he'd have to figure out what to do.

He put the potatoes in a pot of water and set it on the burner. The corn he'd grill with the steaks. He went onto the back porch and loaded the charcoal grill. Jack didn't believe in gas. It has no flavor. No style.

He got the grill going without lighter fluid. He didn't believe in that either. No one wanted to taste accelerant on their meat.

He let the coals do their thing as he went in and got his tongs and other tools. As he worked, his brain slowly, methodically uncoiled the knot of his want. Of his desires.

It was going to be a fun evening, either way.

THIRTY-SEVEN

MEG

SHE WALKED TOWARD THE MAIN road but when she was far enough away from the house and felt no indication of him watching her, she darted back toward the rear of the property.

She wanted to have an idea in her head of what she was dealing with. To know where she was in relation to everything else should things heat up.

"Not *should*," she muttered. "*When*. We both know that this is going to come down to some psychotic battle of the Titans."

She couldn't wait.

His property was big, sprawling, and cluttered, but not messy. The first thing she spotted was an ancient Winnebago. A good place to hide.

"Good."

She opened the door as slowly as she could. Not pulling it fully open. Not wanting the movement to catch Jack's eye should he be watching.

She climbed in. Nothing spectacular. Some spider webs. Some dirt. But it was sealed up well, no sign of critters. She opened a few cabinets. Nada. She lifted the dry-rotted cushions on a bench to find nothing but dust and a few pennies.

More searching. In the cabinet nearest the door, a big can of bear repellent, open and prepped. She shook it. Full.

She investigated further. Found a spool of clothesline. She moved a few things and exited the vehicle.

She kept behind the trees as much as possible and headed toward the big dilapidated barn. When she snuck in between a few missing boards, not having to touch the main door at all, she stopped, staring.

Cars. An automotive graveyard. Mostly old muscle cars. A few jalopies. A tan Ford truck that had seen better days about five decades back.

Everywhere were farming implements. A rake here, a hoe there, a long pole that might have been for fence posting. Small knives, rusted bits of metal, a big beam simply leaning against the wall. There were weapons as far as the eye could see if you knew what you were looking at and what you were doing.

She did her best to study and catalogue.

The loft was intact. The ladder looked sturdy enough. But that was a dead end and wouldn't be smart. Best to know all options, though.

She moved along.

There was a nice barn a few hundred yards away from the car storage. Meg got the feeling it was mostly for show. A safe haven to beckon Jack's guests to get the hunt underway. It held no interest for her.

She went home briefly, freshened up, then walked slowly up to Jack's. Trying to decide, still at this late hour, what she was going to do.

THIRTY-EIGHT

JACK

"**W**EAR SOMETHING PRETTY," HE SAID on a snort. But he found himself changing his jeans and finding a clean blue tee that not only clung to his body in a way that pleased him, but showed off the brightness of his blue eyes.

There was heat in his cheeks and also his crotch. The only other thing that did that for him was hunting. Or hearing someone's pleading screams from the basement or his property.

It had been a while. As far as sex, it had been forever. Prom night. A mere decade and a half ago.

He knew he was an anomaly when it came to sex, but he was also an anomaly when it came to killing. He was a firm believer you could only truly shine at one thing.

When she rapped on the door, his heart skittered in his chest.

Jack found it mildly annoying.

He opened the door and studied her beauty. She'd applied some makeup, but it was a bare minimum. Just enough to give a smoky rim to her eyes and a pale shine to her cheekbones and lips. That was it.

Not whoreish like other girls.

"Come on in. I have to get the steaks off the grill. They only had about two minutes left."

She placed a finger to the very center of his chest, pressing. He felt the pressure in his penis.

"Nice shirt, Jack. Makes your eyes pop."

In his mind, he saw his eyeball popping out of its socket and hoped that wasn't a prediction.

"Thanks." He stepped back, leaving her there in the foyer so he could get the meat.

She followed him. He could hear her moving with nearly silent steps in her Converse sneakers.

She was right behind him when he stepped outside. "Smells good."

"Ribeyes. Hope that's okay."

"That is perfection." She leaned against the side of the house and watched him. "Grill much?"

"Not as much as I should."

"Entertain much?"

"Never. Not for real, anyway."

She grinned at him. In on the joke. That was an odd sensation.

"Had sex once," she said, as if recapping.

"Yep."

"Never with your mother then?"

She kept an utterly straight face. That jaunty eyebrow cocked. Waiting for him to answer. Calmly or otherwise.

"Never. I'm sure plenty of people would think I had. Or wanted to. But I had no desire. Truthfully."

He dropped the steaks on a plate, hung the lid on the side of the grill. It would take a while for those coals to cool down. Jack put the plate on the patio table. Waited.

"How about when you kill them. Do you get off on that? I mean physically."

He stared her in the eye and she never flinched. She didn't look away.

"Yes."

She nodded. Her hands slid into her pockets. She looked both relaxed and alert. She reminded him of a predatory cat.

"And what about you?" he countered.

"I get revved up," she said with a shrug. "And then I want to find someone to fuck."

"But not them?"

She looked up as if recalling. "Once or twice I went there before doing my thing. But it was never as satisfying. It's much better to make them suffer and then find someone else."

"Are you ready to eat?" he asked.

"I am."

He made an after-you gesture and she made it back.

"Don't trust me?"

"Not yet. Maybe never."

"Fair enough."

As he passed her with the plate she asked, "Do you trust me?"

"Not at all," he said.

She laughed.

Dinner was . . . weird. For lack of a better word.

They talked about nothing and everything. How long he'd lived there, why she'd moved, how he made his money, how she made hers. Some similarities there, he noted.

When they were stuffed and simply pushing the remainder of their food around on their plates she said, "How many?"

He knew what she meant but decided to play dumb.

"How many what?"

"Don't fuck with me. You know exactly what I mean. And you

123

know exactly how many. Of course you do."

He speared a baby potato with his fork. "Fifteen," he said.

"When did you start?"

"In earnest?"

"Just when did you start."

"When I was twenty. A game of cat and mouse went too far. I always would date them and chase them. But nothing they could report. I'd asked them if they wanted to play tag or something after making them a nice dinner. A lot of them thought it was sweet. Unusual. You know women are always looking for an unusual date. That was me."

"I bet."

"I liked to hear them scream," he said.

Something flickered across her face.

"And that one? When you were twenty?"

"She flipped out," he said. "Started yelling that I was a lunatic. That she was going to report me to the police. Much like Callie, who you met the other night. Who, by the way, was not my fault."

Meg gave him a nod.

Jack went on, "No matter how many times I told her it had just been a bad joke that had gone awry, she wouldn't hear it. She said she was calling them. Said she'd ignored her instincts that something was off about me. And now she knew she wasn't wrong."

"And you?"

"Broke her neck." He hesitated and then went on anyway. "She didn't die right away. There was time to get her to scream a little more."

"You're being so honest."

It didn't matter, he realized. He could tell her everything because he was going to kill her anyway.

THIRTY-NINE

MEG

HE WAS UNABASHEDLY HIMSELF. HAD been since the beginning. It was what drew her to him. But it was also what repulsed her.

"Why wouldn't I be honest?" he countered.

He sat back in his chair. Tossed his napkin on his plate.

"I don't know. I also know why you would. I'm not a danger to you if you plan to kill me. It's just an observation."

He nodded. "Dessert?"

"What do you have?"

"No booze," he said. "Sorry, I forgot."

He was lying. Meg could feel it in her bones. She nodded. "No worries. I don't need the booze. I *like* the booze. Difference."

"Chocolate cake," he said. "How's that for the world's simplest dessert."

"Simple doesn't mean bad or boring. In fact, it can mean perfection. No chance of overcomplicating it. It is what it is."

She followed him into the kitchen carrying both their plates.

She had a moment where she vividly saw herself bringing the edge of one down onto his skull, cleaving it, opening a gusher of blood that would be like a red ribbon unwinding from his unzipped skin.

Instead, she scraped them in the kitchen trash and then put them in the sink, stacked neatly.

He got the cake out of the fridge and two plates from the cabinet. He fished two forks out of the drawer. Jack moved to return to the table.

Meg said, "What about outside? We could eat the cake out in the evening air. It's not too stifling tonight."

He nodded, following her out the door. She allowed herself to turn her back on him, a show of trust.

They sat. The light from the kitchen spilled across the table. Dusk was settling in, not fully yet, but the light had purpled.

"What about you? What made you put a bullet in Cupcake's brain?"

She took a bite of cake, surprised to find it very good. She even liked the fact it was chilled.

"I was raped when I was twelve by three older boys. One had been a friend previously."

"I'm sorry," Jack said.

She couldn't stop it. She heard herself snort. "I doubt that."

Jack set his fork down. "I'm a killer not a rapist."

"Is there much of a difference?"

"Yes, I've never raped anyone."

She inclined her head.

"You're a killer. Have you ever raped anyone?" he asked.

"No. Of course not."

Not unless you count fucking one of the worst of my worst in the ass with a broom handle. Then maybe . . .

She kept that to herself.

"Then you see the difference."

"I suppose." She took another bite of cake, licked the fork clean.

Jack shook his head. "Rape is so . . ."

He put his fork down. Took a moment to straighten his napkin, smoothing it out. A nervous habit, perhaps?

Didn't matter.

Meg plunged her fork into his hand. Felt the tines hit weathered wood beneath.

She got to hear Jack scream. It was pretty sweet, she had to admit.

The sweetness only lasted a moment and then she was on her feet because so was he. Eyes wide, anger there, shock, surprise, admiration, even.

He moved toward her, barreling fast, and, as he did, she bobbed and got up under his arm, the fork dangling by one tine in his hand. She bum rushed him into the grill, pressed his face to the grate. She had to put all her weight behind it. It wasn't as hot as it had been, but she felt heat baking off it. Heard the cold meat sizzle of his cheek pressing the grate.

This time Jack howled.

She shivered. Her skin erupting in goosebumps. She looked around for a better weapon because her hands weren't free to get into her pocket.

He was big, strong, and slippery like an eel.

Her pondering fucked her in the ass because he kicked back with his foot and took her leg out. Nothing broke, she knew that, but her leg folded like a broken lawn chair.

She hissed, clutched her knee, and had just enough time to roll to her back and out of the way as Jack came at her with a barbecue fork.

His face was charred, black skin with raw red flesh peeking through. His eyebrow was singed. His face a mask of rage.

She backpedaled as the tips of the big fork hit the deck where she'd just been.

"You'd better fucking run," he snarled. "Or sit still so I can gut

GO DOWN HARD

you like a fish."

She kicked out, connected weakly with his ankle. But it was enough that he wobbled.

She skittered across the deck, loping like a wild dog, and took off into the darkness of his playground.

GO DOWN HARD

FORTY

JACK

HIS HAND THROBBED LIKE A rotten tooth. His face was indescribable. The pain was whatever lay beyond hot. It felt like it was still cooking. Because it was.

Two thoughts went through his mind simultaneously. This was going to make it harder for him to woo women. And he had to kill this bitch. His respect and admiration for her as a mutual predator had fled.

His interest in fucking her had as well. Which pleased him. He was not a rapist.

So, as he pounded down the hill after her, making sure to never look away so he was completely sure where she went, he decided he'd strangle her. Slowly. Making it last. Giving her air and time to regroup before returning to the slow restriction of her oxygen.

He could practically smell the death on her.

"I'm coming for you. I'm going to make you scream for me," he growled.

She heard him, he could tell by how her shoulders hunched

suddenly, but she made absolutely no sound. None. He could barely hear her ragged breath because his own was drowning it out. There was an odd whistling coming from his cheek but he couldn't stop to think about that now.

She darted left toward the old barn and he grinned, the cool night air a blessing on his seared face.

He loved the barn. Run. Run, little Meg, into the barn.

He slowed down a little, caught his breath, watching the door bump open even briefly to admit her. He could take a breath. She was inside with all the cars. In the dark. Finding her way around. Thinking she might be safe for a moment.

That was her mistake. She'd never be safe from him. She might play with her little dates and torture them. Kill them, even. But he doubted she'd ever met the likes of him.

He bent and put his hands on his knees, took a moment to catch his breath. His face thrummed in time with his pulse. The wound in his hand a bizarre backup singer to the main act.

His mouth tasted like fire and pain. His head pounded. He'd have paid any amount of money for a cold fucking rag.

He pressed his hand to his ruined cheek and had to stifle the urge to scream. The only thing that would even come close to making that thing feel better was feeling her life bleed away under his hands.

He tugged the barn door. The wood was so dry rotted it barely weighed a thing. He knew how far to pull it open so it didn't squeak. Dusk was dying a slow death. There was just enough light to make shadows pop—black against lavender.

He slipped through the crack, stood there, waited. He took a breath, ears straining to hear her. He listened so hard he could hear his own ears ringing ridiculously from the adrenaline and pain.

Nothing.

He took another step inside. Close to the Chevy Impala. No

noise.

He took another step.

He heard a rustling. A small sound, hard to pinpoint. It didn't sound like it was coming from the right or the left. It was oddly muddled.

Another step. He held his breath. Waited.

And then his feet went out from under him. He hit the ground so hard his teeth smacked together. He spit, feeling a small shard of tooth shoot out of his mouth as he did. She was under the car. And she was armed.

He had time to register that before she jabbed at him with whatever implement she held.

There was enough light to make her out under there, grinning, panting. Jabbing again. It was a hoe, he saw. He had to move.

His stunned body didn't want to.

The hoe hit his ankle, bent it. Jack backpedaled on his elbows. He pulled himself out of her way and struggled to his feet. His blood lust had surpassed anything he'd ever felt before. His instinct to find her and beat her until she stopped breathing.

He heard her scurry from under the car, moving through the dirt and clutter. Worse than any barn rat he'd ever seen.

He snarled, infuriated. He darted toward where he thought she was and his abused ankle threatened to dump him on his ass.

He kept moving forward, but not before stopping to grab something—anything—to have as a weapon. His hand closed around something metal and wood. He held it up and saw it was a rusted pair of clippers. Perfect. He muscled them open and moved toward the last place he'd spotted her. Or thought he'd spotted her.

She'd kept low, ducking and hunching behind the cars. Slouching around his barn like she owned the fucking place.

It was fine, he assured himself. She'd simply caught him off guard. It wouldn't happen again.

FORTY-ONE

MEG

SHE WANTED TO SUCK AIR like a whirlpool. Instead, she forced herself to sip it.

He was coming. She could see his shadow moving among the other shadows. Her heart raced, her blood rushed, and she could admit to herself that her pulse, at the moment, beat heaviest between her thighs.

Because she just wanted to fucking kill him.

Kill him.

Kill.

Him.

It raced through her head like a catchy commercial jingle.

She held the hoe in her right hand, clung to the barn ladder with her left arm. She looped it through the rungs to ensure she wouldn't inadvertently slip and fall.

She was about six rungs up, which would allow her to either retreat up to the loft or drop down and run. It felt like a good option.

He crept toward her general vicinity. She could see him turning his head left and right. Looking. Which meant, though he was headed toward her, he wasn't headed *right* toward her. He wasn't sure where she was.

Which was in her favor.

She waited. Watching. Doing her best to stay completely silent.

He turned and she saw he had something. Some sort of weapon or a stick or a broom maybe. Something. He was armed.

She wasn't dumb enough to think she'd bested him. She'd gotten lucky. Everything had turned out in her favor so far. But it could change at any moment.

Some writer she'd liked years before—name long forgotten—had posted her personal motto online. "Never buy your own hype." Meg had adopted that as a motto for life.

She wouldn't consider herself victorious until his heart stopped beating. And then she'd still wait for that Freddy Krueger, Jason Voorhees, Michael Myers moment where he'd spring back to life.

Meg waited.

He got closer and she saw they were shears. Or at the very least, something with a blade. She'd need to be careful. Aim well. And get it right on the first go.

Her heart rate was ridiculous. She wouldn't be surprised if she had a fucking stroke and keeled over up there, entwined around the ladder rungs like some bizarre homicidal vine. Tom Petty was right. Waiting *was* the hardest part.

Finally, after what seemed like a year, he was close enough. Standing right below her, not much more than a foot away. He held the shears defensively but had no idea she lurked above him.

She felt a swell of satisfaction and stifled it. Getting cocky got you killed.

He stood there, waiting, watching, breathing.

Finally, Meg was as brave as she was going to get. Now or

133

never. Before he moved along thinking he'd missed her.

"Psst—"

He automatically looked up and she did her best one-handed croquet swing. Summers being forced to play that asinine game in the Baltimore city heat and swelter had to count for something.

She connected the hoe to the back of his head and gave it all her might.

It wasn't as strong as she'd hoped. The old ladder creaked and wavered and she had to adjust her grip at the last moment because it felt like it was going to go, collapse under her like a pile of sticks.

But the hit was hard enough he went down on his face, his shears skittering across the barn floor and hitting something metallic with a hollow *bong*.

Meg jumped down.

"Fuck!" he bellowed and she knew he'd gone down but hadn't gone out.

She misjudged how close she was as she bolted past him, headed for the gap in the barn walls where boards were missing and meager light shone in. The outside was barely lighter than the inside but it was something to see by, at least.

He snagged her ankle and she went down on that bad knee. His grip was strong and she could hear his free arm flailing around on the floor—searching for those shears, no doubt.

He managed a hearty yank and pulled her backwards toward him.

Meg refused to scream but she hissed "shit" under her breath. She'd dropped the hoe and couldn't quite snag it. The handle about an inch too far from her straining fingers.

She kicked back and felt her sneaker slam against his jaw.

He shouted and she did it again.

The hand on her ankle relaxed for just a second. She felt it snap toward her—grabbing—as she scrambled forward. She shoved herself through the gaps in the barn side and hurried out into the night.

She had no doubt Jack was right behind her. Good. Let him come.

FORTY-TWO

JACK

CUNT.

He reserved that word for special occasions.

His mother, had she heard him say it, would have laid into him with her giant wooden kitchen paddle. Then she'd have force fed him a bar of soap.

It was okay to kill women, but not use that word.

He struggled to get to his feet and every moment of pain and hardship honed his rage. He stood there, swaying, waiting for the barn to stop moving. His ears whistled like a teapot, his head felt like it was vibrating. Two of his teeth were loose and he could feel dirt and debris clinging to his freshly burned skin.

When he ran his hand through his hair, it came away wet with blood. She'd possibly opened the back of his head like a tin can.

"Cunt," he said aloud. This time giving birth to the epithet with his voice.

He managed one staggering step and had to steady himself with a hand on the hood of the car closest to him.

He couldn't find his shears, but he did find a baseball bat.

"Perfect," he garbled.

Head injury? Possibly. But fuck it. That bitch had to die.

His sole purpose now was a burning passion to watch her suffer.

He bolstered his mood and motivated himself with the image of choking her again. Watching her face turn red, then purple, then eventually blue as her oxygen was cut off. All his favorite colors. Then he'd keep her around until she turned gray to make sure she was truly gone.

She had a horseshoe up her ass, that was for sure.

No, you liked her. And that was your fatal flaw. You wanted her and that is never good. Mother taught you that.

He made his way to the barn door, using the Louisville Slugger as more of a cane than a weapon. Whatever. He would adjust, adapt, survive.

There was no way Meg was going to take him out and best him on his own goddamn property. In his own hunting ground.

"No," he snarled.

Hobbling out the door, he forced himself to walk as normally as possible. Trying very hard to right his equilibrium.

He stood there, panting, and tried to get his breathing to stabilize.

He heard a bang-thud-bounce. Cocked his head. Even with his ears ringing he knew that sound. What the fuck was it?

He leaned heavily on the bat to steady himself. It might be time to admit, to himself, at least, that Meg might have knocked him for a loop with that blow to the head.

"You're fine, you baby," he said. He could almost hear his mother saying it to him. She never did abide giving up or capitulating to hardships.

He shut his eyes and immediately opened them. Not a good idea. The world moved too much when his eyes were shut.

GO DOWN HARD

The upside to vertigo was it distracted him from the pain in his cheek. That whistling was still there, though, and it unnerved him.

The wind blew and he heard it again. That bang-thud-bounce.

His brain gave it up then. It was the door to the Winnebago that never quite latched fully. She'd gone in there. And now it was banging every time the wind blew.

He started that way. It was slow going, but he managed. As he got closer, his blood got up. Singing in his veins. The hunger to hear her screams was almost overwhelming.

"Here, pretty pretty pretty . . ."

He paused outside the door and waited. There was a furtive scraping. A whimper. Maybe he'd done some damage to that knee after all. He smiled.

He wanted to rush in, yank the door open, enter, but was hesitant. That infuriated him.

He'd never been afraid of *any* woman with the exception of his mother. And aren't all boys afraid of their mothers?

He took a deep breath and let his body settle.

He clung to the baseball bat and stepped up on the metal landing that led to the inside of the RV. He steadied himself again.

Then the door burst open and he was falling . . .

FORTY-THREE

MEG

SHE WAITED. SHE COULD HEAR him. Her heart felt like a fish flopping through its last breaths in her chest.

She was right behind the warped old door. Something she'd never understood about RVs. How some of the doors tended to open out. But in this instance, that was an excellent thing.

It had taken him for-fucking-ever to get to the RV. So, he'd either had trouble figuring out where she'd gone or he was moving slow.

Given the blow to the head and then the kicks to the face, she was betting on the latter.

But you never knew, so she was prepared to face a fully functional Jack.

She put too much weight on that one knee and pain skittered through it. She'd be able to run if she had to but, by God, she hoped she didn't.

She waited, holding her breath, listening to her heart bang. Then the Winnebago tilted ever so slightly. She felt it dip. Instead of opening the door and then stepping up, he'd stepped up to open the door. Giving her the element of total surprise.

She took it. Gleefully.

Meg shoved with all her might, slamming her shoulder into the aluminum door as she forced it wide.

She heard a startled grunt and then a growl. The RV shook again and she could hear his meaty thud as he hit the ground outside the mobile home.

She was trapped though. The only bad point. She'd tried the front doors when she'd first entered, but they wouldn't open. Something she'd neglected to check earlier in the day.

She moved farther back into the darkness of the vehicle. With a bum knee, she wasn't sure she had it in her to put on enough speed to rush past him, and a quick peak out the window with its threadbare curtains barely more stable than cobwebs, verified he was indeed right at the foot of the step.

He was struggling to his feet. Moving slow. He had some kind of crutch.

Meg slammed the palm of her hand to her mouth to stifle the giddy laughter wanting to rise up out of her like carbonation bubbles.

He was really fucked up. And she'd done that. Her glee flowed through her veins like a drug.

She did her best to ignore it because, she knew as well as anyone, how quickly the tables could turn.

He was almost fully upright now and took the thing he had and beat it against his palm. He swayed slightly—a good sign—but then did it again.

"I'm coming for you, you horrible cunt," he barked. He said it good and loud. Clearly unafraid anyone but Meg would hear it.

The hair on the nape of her neck stood on end.

She rummaged around.

She only had moments before he came in. If she was going to

make this work, she'd have to work fast because the Winnie was close quarters and she was pretty sure what Jack was holding was a bat.

Slow or not, he was pissed. Using the word cunt was something she'd lay money on him rarely doing. He'd think it rude or something. To say Jack was angry was the understatement of the year.

She worked fast, with trembling fingers. Part fear, part adrenaline, part excitement.

FORTY-FOUR

JACK

THIS WAS GETTING FUCKING RIDICULOUS. It was his fault, really. He should have seen that coming. He should have treated that door as if it was possibly rigged with explosives. Meg was not one of his simpering, begging, screeching guests. She wasn't like those B-movie scream queen victims. Meg was somewhat like him. More from an event that changed her than nature, but that could make someone even more formidable.

He beat the bat against the ground to try and get his nerve up. He yelled to her again: "Unless you have that stupid little pea shooter of yours, Meg, you better be wary of me. I've had just about enough of this . . ."

How many times had his mother yelled that to him as she came searching through the house for him with his father's left-behind belt?

He'd never known anything of his father except the bite of his brown leather belt.

He moved toward the RV as steadily as he could in case she was watching. But it was a hard thing to do. His cheek was sizzling like he'd just laid it back on the grill. His head throbbed. He could feel thick blood running down the back of his neck and his jaw felt like it was hanging funny.

His words came out monstrous. As if his mouth was malformed. Thanks to her, it very well may be.

"I'm coming for you, bitch!" he roared.

Then, partly to work up his nerve and partly to put some fear into the seemingly fearless woman, he beat the merry hell out of the door to the RV.

Only when he felt too exhausted to even advance onto the step did Jack get control of himself.

By then the door was hanging on by one hinge.

He yanked it open, flinched, embarrassed of his fear. Then he took the step as steadily as he was able. Which, at this point, wasn't much. He pushed the bat into the yawning doorway, fast, then withdrew it. Hoping to hit her if she was lurking there. The bat cleared, encountering nothing but air, and he exhaled. He moved inside another foot after waving the bat to the left.

Nothing.

She was in here, though. He'd disabled the front doors of the RV ages ago. The back door was covered over with plywood on the inside. Dead end.

And for her it would be. This would be her dead end.

"Where are you, Meg? Don't play coy now."

He stood there, heaving breath, trying to ignore the symphony of pain saturating every cell of his body. "Where are you, you fucking whore?"

His mouth. My god. It was getting away from him today.

He heard something and froze. He was being a bad hunter. Forgetting all his skills. You can't hear your prey if you're shooting your mouth off.

143

He held his breath and strained to hear.

Rustling. Very faint. By the back of the RV. All the way back behind the bench seat that bracketed the table. It all folded down into a bed for camping.

She was hiding back there.

He smiled. It hurt his entire upper body to do it, but he did it anyway.

She'd gotten the better of him so far, but not any longer. He'd gotten his head together and was ready to do this the way he always did it. Logically, with skill and ease.

He gathered the shred of energy he had and used the bat to propel himself. He was almost to her, coming at a good clip, when the world turned roughly. He went down on his gut, his teeth clacking together yet again. He bit his tongue so hard he felt a chunk of it drop off.

Tripwire, his brain snickered.

Fucking tripwire.

He was too stunned to yell. He simply let out some wounded animal sound. A bear being slowly gutted maybe.

His brains scrambled, his vision wavering, spots of glowing fire appeared in his darkened vision.

"You . . . whore . . ."

He was at a loss to be more creative. He gripped the bat that thankfully hadn't rolled away, still very aware that to get to the only exit she'd have to go past him. And he'd be ready for her.

He sat up, snarling, drool rolling out of his mouth. Who knew where the fuck the tip of his tongue was. Who cared! He just wanted to deal with her.

When he sat up, the fire in his head suddenly tripled. And Jack couldn't make any noise. At all.

FORTY-FIVE

MEG

THE STREAM HIT HIM IN the face so hard it drove him back a few steps. She made sure to keep her tank top pulled up over her face. Did her best to exhale and not draw any air in.

Silence at first. Inexplicable dead silence. Then a moan that seemed to come from the center of him. Then it started.

"Jesus! My eyes!" Jack was paddling on the floor, arms and legs moving like he was swimming, but he wasn't. He wasn't trying to crawl either. He was simply writhing in pain.

His hand came up to his eyes and cupped them, but that seemed to make it worse.

"My throat!" He was gargling and heaving. He turned his head and puked up his dinner.

The smell hit Meg and her stomach rolled.

She was eyeing her own tripwire, Jack, and his proximity to the bat.

She'd have to make a break for it soon before he got his wits about him.

He'd hunched back on his knees like he was attempting some impromptu yoga and moving into child's pose. He cupped his eyes, thrust his hands out, cupped them again, repeating the motion over and over again. Because nothing was comfortable and nothing helped.

Her brain tuned back into his screaming.

"If I'm fucking blind I'm coming to kill you," he bellowed. He turned his head, puked up some drool. His eyes streamed with tears, his throat worked with the effort to breathe.

Bear repellent. Who knew?

"So far you haven't done so well with the killing me thing." She said it softly to make sure he couldn't pinpoint her very well. She wanted to get past him.

He sat up on his knees, eyes swollen to slits, red, weeping. He looked like some deranged prairie dog.

A wave of hysterical laughter rippled out of her mouth and he turned toward the sound, infuriated and clearly personally offended.

This made her laugh harder.

"Bitch," he ground out. Gagged. Spit. Then vomited again.

Meg moved toward him, eyeing the rope she'd tied tight between the bench and the small RV sink.

She needed to clear him and her own booby trap. She'd pulled at the plywood in the back of the vehicle but it was glued down well despite its age and wouldn't budge. She had to get past him to get out.

Another step and he froze, moving his head back and forth like an animal scenting the wind.

"Worried now, Meg? I'm blocking the exit."

She thought to climb up on the table and possibly jump down over him and the rope but he somehow knew and grabbed the bat, waving it before him viciously. The RV was comfortable for traveling, but still a tight fit. No way would she escape a blow from the bat if she went that way.

She grabbed the bear repellent to hit him with another stream but the trigger jammed. She shook it, tried again, and still nothing.

"Uh-oh. No more fire juice to hide behind."

Meg took a deep breath and backpedaled three steps. He moved to accommodate, trying to track her by sound.

The moment he turned slightly to the right, she barreled toward him on the left.

She pushed off hard to clear the taut rope and just as she approached it, he grabbed her and she was falling.

She went down hard, landing on that knee again. Of course. She screamed and he laughed.

His grip on her was hard. His fingers rigid like bone. The fumes of the bear spray came off him in nearly visible waves and she gagged from the closeness.

"Not pleasant, is it?" he snarled in her face. His face no longer the handsome, lanky boy next door. Now he looked like something out of a horror movie. Face blackened and open at the cheek, drool and blood and vomit leaking from his mouth, eyes swollen nearly shut. His hair was a mess, he smelled, he was so sweaty and slick with repellent it was like wrestling an eel.

She kneed him in the crotch and he went still, air escaping him. She allowed herself a breath. Which is why she didn't see the punch coming. The uppercut rattled her brain and her teeth. Her ears erupted with a concerto of ringing.

She scrambled away from him and tried to move past him but he took the bat, choked up on it, and hit her in the bad knee.

Meg screamed and, on the inhale, got a snoot full of the pepper spray. She started to cough, scrambling on the floor, trying to get her knees under her, scratching and punching as much as she could.

147

She managed to get herself turned around and began to crawl to the door.

Jack had gotten up on his knees partway. He was swinging blindly, but in the confines of the walkway, he was landing his blows.

The bat came down against the back of her thighs and she screamed. She couldn't help it.

"There it is. That's what I like to hear," he growled. "You have a lovely scream. I knew you would." Then he retched again and she managed to get a few feet by soldier crawling.

He landed another blow along the back of her calves and she gritted her teeth, bit her tongue, whimpered, but refused to scream for him.

"Oh, don't hold out on me," he snarled. She moved forward a little more and he grabbed her by the ankle. Her legs throbbed from mid-thigh to ankle. She had no idea if he'd done any damage but it hurt.

He wouldn't let go. The door was so much closer now. She could hear the crickets outside. The sound of freedom.

"Where are you going?" he asked. He was having fun now. Despite the pain in what looked like every part of him, he was enjoying this.

That pissed her off. She reared back, hooked her fingers, and dug her fingertips into the ruined mess of his cheek. She pushed hard into the raw meat of his face.

Jack bayed like a dying dog. He let loose like nothing she'd ever heard.

"I'm going out!" she said when he buckled under the pain she'd just inflicted. She moved as fast as she could on hands and questionable knees toward the door.

She was right on the lip when Jack's body weight hit her. Her head was out the RV door, the rest of her trapped inside with him.

FORTY-SIX

JACK

GOD THAT HAD BEEN BEAUTIFUL. Despite all the pain. That scream, that had made him hard.

He hit her with the best tackle he could muster. Which was shit. Utter shit. But it stopped her. They hovered right there on the threshold of the RV. She wiggled and squirmed, but hadn't uttered a single scream since the last one.

Sad.

He pinched her. He didn't know what he was pinching, but he pinched it as hard as he could. Trying to pinch a piece off. Grinding his fingers together, tugging, pulling.

She growled beneath her breath but didn't scream.

He pulled her hair. Hard enough that a chunk of it came away in his hand.

"What's wrong? You don't like it all up close and personal like this?" He snagged another piece. Pulled.

Still she didn't scream.

Infuriating.

GO DOWN HARD

He bent his head and bit her. He thought it was her neck but in the tangled chaos it was hard to tell. He kept biting until he tasted blood, and yet, she stayed silent.

Then she hit him with an elbow to the face and his head rang like a bell, made worse when that tipped them, together as a single unit, out the front door. They tumbled down the single aluminum step and landed hard in the packed dirt beneath.

He was sprawled mostly on top of her, pinning her body. In the cold September moonlight, through slitted eyes, he could see where he'd bitten her. He could see bruises on her face.

He gulped in a breath. Then another. She was regrouping too. No one moved. Everyone exhausted.

"I personally like the up close and personal," he said.

Then she hit him with a rock and he went down for a second. Normally that wouldn't do him in, Jack consoled himself as the world blacked out for a moment, but it had been a rough night.

FORTY-SEVEN

MEG

AND HERE SHE WAS. JUST like when she was a kid. Cut, hurt, running through the woods away from a boy. But was she?

Meg got to the biggest tree in the field and waited. He'd come. She knew he would. He wanted to kill her so damn bad. The thought that she was any different than the others was gone now. She might be like him, but he still wanted to hear her scream, then end her life.

She caught her breath. Her knee throbbed. The other would probably be fine, but the right one was fucked. She'd have to baby it, possibly pay the doc a visit, which she hated.

Her neck thumped in time with her heart. The fucker had bitten her. She could feel it like some sort of radioactive bite from a comic book.

Too bad she was already a killer. It would have been a much better story had his bite turned her into one.

She heard him coming before she saw him. The thud-pause-thud-pause of him hobbling up the hill with his baseball bat. The whistling of his breath. She was fairly certain the whistling was the air moving *through* his ruined cheek. He kept pausing to wipe his eyes.

And yet he came. The monster from the horror story, the villain from the movie. And she had to respect the hell out of that. Because she would have done the same thing.

He crested the hill and she dropped a rock. So he could hear.

Then the speed came, catching her off guard. He barreled at her, bat brandished like some sword in a medieval fight.

He hit her full force and she went down, the air going out of her. His bat had skittered away, but Jack had a backup plan. His hands crept around her throat. Despite all his injuries, fury fueled him. He squeezed and the world went sparkly at the edges.

She kicked up and tried to get her hand in her pocket. She should have thought that out better.

He squeezed and she gagged. She brought her knee up into his crotch and that bought her a loosening of his grip, a sip of air, and her hand finally slid into her pocket.

His grip returned and she found herself lightheaded. Clutching her weapon but without the energy to use it. Oh, the irony.

She gave him another knee to the groin and it landed better this time. He sagged, his hands stayed but his grip weakened.

She brought the glass up to his throat, pressed. He stilled. She had his attention.

"It was a great first and only date," she said, her voice as exhausted as the rest of her. "And I agree. I also prefer it up close and personal like this."

She smiled at him and drove the glass into his throat, the soft part, beneath his chin. She pushed it in so fast and hard she sliced her fingertips. Just like she had once upon a time on a deserted street after school. She hit it with the heel of her hand to make sure it went deep as possible. It sank so deep only a bare wink of green glass was visible in the moonlight.

Jack looked like he wanted to reply. Like he had a witty come-back. Instead, he gargled like a clogged drain and baptized her with hot, sticky blood.

She lay there for a moment, thinking how close it was to how she'd have lain post sex. She sprawled there with him draped over her as the last flickers and clicks of motion passed through him.

Then she rolled him off, grabbed his bat, and used it as a crutch for her long trek home.

FORTY-EIGHT

MEG

SHE POURED HERSELF A WHISKEY. Fuck two or three fingers, she filled the tumbler to the top. She drank half of it immediately and then hobbled to the shower. She turned it on as hot and as hard as she could stand it.

She stripped her clothes, put them in the trash can. She'd burn them later.

She took another swig of booze and then climbed gingerly into the shower. She let the hot water pour over her, rinsing her. Then she scrubbed her hair. Her body. She stood there, cooking herself to lobster red beneath the boiling spray.

She toweled off, finished off the drink, and cleaned and dressed the bite mark. It was fairly deep.

There were black marks on her hip already where he'd pinched and blooming bruises on her thighs and calves.

She peered out the window with a brand-new drink, raised it, and smiled. "You were a good adversary, Jack. But no more innocent women for you. Rest well."

A flicker of shadowy movement in the yard caught her attention. Was this the 'killer won't die' moment? The hand popping up from the grave scene? She stared for a moment then smiled and opened the door. She whistled to Casey. He came to her immediately.

"Come in, handsome. Hungry?"

He beat his tail steadily and nuzzled her hand when she offered it. She put down a bowl of water and gave him some lunch meat. She'd get food tomorrow. She had a dog now.

Her phone burbled on the table and she wandered over feeling loose and warm from the booze. Maybe she'd make herself a pack of noodles. Her energy was low.

"Hi there. I hope you remember me. Michael Flay. I was just checking in to see if we could still meet soon."

"Oh, Michael. You are an eager boy, aren't you? Men like you . . . what am I gonna do with you?"

She tapped away carefully now that the buzz from the booze had hit.

"Hi, Michael. I'm busy for a few nights. Hurt myself running. But you do seem my type. How's the night after tomorrow sound? Can't wait to meet."

ACKNOWLEDGEMENTS

Firstly, thanks to Jason, my biggest, hairiest cheerleader. His love of horror rekindled mine and eventually led to this book. Secondly, to my daughter Sydney. A writer in her own right, she's the one to ask the hard plot questions. The real stumpers. And finally, to my son Ian. The boy who'd willingly watch all my beloved B movies with me. The cheesier the better.

And obviously, thank you to C.V. Hunt for plucking this book out of the submission pile (plus a bad ass cover) and to Andersen Prunty for his editing. I'd like to give him a dollar for every "that" he deleted, but I don't have that kind of money.

For the last fifteen years, Ali Seay has written professionally under a pen name. Now she's running amok and writing as herself in the genre she's always loved the most. She lives in Baltimore with her family. Her greatest desire is to own a vintage Airstream and hit the road.

Other Grindhouse Press Titles

Made in the USA
Monee, IL
21 December 2021